BLOODHARVEST

BLOODHARVEST

PART 1 OF ELEGY IN PALLAS

MATTHEW MILLER

Printed in the United States of America

First Printing: 2018

ISBN 978-0-9600099-0-9

Leibniz Clockwork
PO Box 124122
Lakewood, CO 80214

www.leibnizclockwork.com

Special thanks to Andrew Ough and Patrice Delva.

CONTENTS

♦

The Contract

Her Elvish Majesty solicited me to rescue her son, Aehr, from the goblin fortress of Bloodharvest. Elves tended to rely on humans for such things. I was lying through my teeth to get a better contract.

"Your appearance is not one that insinuates 'divine cosmic power,'" admitted the Surrogate for Her Majesty. He was a delicate elf with tall features. Everything about him, from height to facial structure, was stretched upward, an oddity as he was only neck-tall on me. He had power though. The purse was his to control. Her Majesty didn't lower herself to mundane details like her son being kidnapped by goblins—asinine—so while she sat right here, she didn't say anything if ever her Surrogate spoke first. I didn't like either of them, but he had all the money.

"You grossly misinterpret my dress, translating it into the language of earthly desires," I replied. "It is because I am devoted to cosmic powers that I care nothing for your mundane things."

I look shadier than a petting hole on a box of scorpions. I was dressed in a mix of browns and black, with a tight undershirt and several layers of loose wrappings. My reversible cloak, forest green and granite gray, hung from the back of my chair, and my boots were stitched together from three different animals on a substrate of undyed wool. I wore nine belts. My shirt hung like moss. There wasn't a clean outline on me; everything blurred together. My clothing defeats the eye, but in an office that defeat is unpleasant to look on. This time I wasn't wearing face paint, and my face was the only part of me that looked like a woman instead of cut-and-paste shadow.

Her Majesty met me in a green-and-black room with jade furnishings on ebony tiles. Nothing ran straight. The floor crested to my left and sank into a gentle depression by the door. Her Majesty reclined at an angle on the royal couch, leaning ever so slightly to her left, toward the Surrogate. Her spine curved her body to the side arch of the chair. Whales spouted in relief on armrests that bored like roots from the back to the seat. She was dressed regally, stinking of royalty and money in long robes that lay warm against her skin. The arc of her elvish hip was insinuated by sea-foam silk. We could not be more different.

Beside her the Surrogate was doing a human impersonation. He sat upright, which looked wrong for an elf but correct because I was a human. The combination was distinctly uncomfortable to look at and had to be equally uncomfortable to do. His back was harpoon-straight. The chair wasn't flat, but he contorted himself to verticality by will. Between him and me was a desk, each leg a palm trunk, the broad fronds woven together with anchoring gold to make a flat surface. It was lacquered in something that smelled of sandalwood.

"Hmm." The Surrogate pressed his lips together. "As mundane realms are my own concern, I cannot accede to your requests."

"Alas, only I stand between Aehr and a terrible fate. Of course, you could mobilize the army and lay siege to the Polyp. I hear that the Warlord Dread did so, leading armies of men without number against it during the reign of Kuranes the Seventh. He won in a mere three years."

The Surrogate opened his mouth, then halted, like I'd snatched the words from his lips.

I went on. "That was under Kuranes the Terrible, whose unstoppable armies ruined Pallas's face until the gods themselves rose up against him. No one has matched his reign. However, if he was able to succeed in three years, you could no doubt do the same. Aehr is young. Maybe time does not concern you." We humans were expected to be coarse. We didn't understand deep feelings or emotions. Every elf knew it. I kept my expression serious. If I sold this, and if they believed the worst of me, they would take it at face value that I actually didn't understand how bad years of torture at goblin hands could be and earnestly expected a mostly pastoral nation to match the military exploits of humanity's greatest, if arguably evilest, conqueror. They would be bargaining for haste against my ignorant patience. I didn't tell them there were only a few weeks to get to Bloodharvest and make it work, because I wanted them to negotiate for something I already wanted to do.

I tried to look innocent, earnest, and mildly stupid. Not too stupid, of course, because I still wanted them to believe I could do it. Naive but cunning.

"And I have been to Bloodharvest before," I added.

"Yes. We heard." The Surrogate bit the words apart.

The queen flushed and looked imploringly at her Surrogate. She wanted to throw the house at me right now.

"Your terms are odd," he said, pointedly ignoring her. How lofty of him. "You want the option to sell ten trade cargoes of winter wheat at nine over seven Celephian marks."

"Just the option," I agreed.

"Just an option," the Surrogate repeated. His elvish eyes lifted at the corners. When he squinted, he looked furious and suspicious.

"Who among us can foresee the stars? Why would we delve into their realm and think ourselves natives of the heavens, we who exist on grim Pallas? I leave the future to them, merely desiring the opportunity to attain my own ends." I raised my hands heavenward, resigning my fate to the stars above.

"It is such an odd request," admitted Her Majesty, for the first time breaking her silence.

Her Majesty was between the Surrogate and me in height, somewhere between me and the moon in wealth. She was a lovely person. It drove me crazy. She was so weak.

"It is what the powers above ask of me," I replied.

"Miss Elegy—" began the Surrogate. I cut him off immediately.

"Excuse me. Astrologamage Elegy." Elves are twitchy about titles. They append them to names, building people out of appellations with apostrophes and hyphens.

They're also far more aware than most humans of being interrupted, so my interjection into the Surrogate's response was astounding in and of itself, even with my politeness. The title called for it. If the Surrogate got started building his wall around me as 'Miss Elegy,' I might as well go back to the little girls' table. He could either take the title or address the interruption, and they hate reliving rudeness by addressing it.

"Astrologamage Elegy," repeated the Surrogate. He tasted each rancid syllable. "This option is most unpleasant. We must acknowledge that you may fulfill the contract if it is in your best interests to do so, but will fail to do so if it is in ours."

"Yes," I agreed.

"You profit on both ends of the deal."

"I do."

"At our expense."

"At the expense of the goblin kingdoms! They will be deprived of their foul practices, and the noble prince Aehr will be home to lead the halls of Elvendom to new fertility. Think of the joy he will bring to the land! The people hang banners to mourn his absence. How they will rejoice in his return!" I could have gone on, but I paused. Her Majesty was hooked, nodding along as her heart broke. The Surrogate had already decided my demesne abutted Mermogan's castle in the Dark Abyss.

Her Majesty rustled her robes faintly. I could put so much leverage on someone by threatening them with their kidnapped child. It was terrible. Truly reprehensible of me. I forgave myself.

The Surrogate blinked first. His heart was hard as mine, but he had duties to the queen.

"It will be done," he said.

"Splendid! You already have my boilerplate. Summon me to sign the contract when it is complete, and—"

"It is already done," interrupted the Surrogate. He had the contract ready. "When can you leave, Astrologamage Elegy?"

Oh damn. That's what a pissed elf sounds like. Interestingly, only humans swear.

I took the contract and read it.

I'd learned about options in Celephias, that den of drug-dealing necromancers, money worshippers, and generally horrible people. I loved them, but I would never live there. I do take a few weeks on the Isle every now and then, though, just to find out what the serious miscreants are up to. I may be bad, but they've institutionalized it. Options practice is a fascinating bit of financial black magic. They buy and sell options for everything, in many cases with greater enthusiasm than they buy and sell the actual contracts underlying the options. What I learned from all that is that there's more money to be made in possibilities than in certainty.

I smiled as I read. It looked straightforward. The contract only went into force on the return of Prince Aehr. It laid out quality and quantity explicitly. They specified the wheat buyer. They named the option expiration date four times. The elves had obviously tried to think of everything, and coming from first causes, they did a good job. Yet my boilerplate remained.

Still smiling, I said, "I can leave tonight at sunset. Your Majesty"—if I called her 'Your Majesty' I could skip three breaths of 'Eminent Lady of the Crystal Halls,' yadda yadda—"you have my word, I will return with your son or die trying. My kind trade on our names. You may reference it."

"Thank you," said Her Majesty.

The Surrogate bustled me up and out, and didn't waste a lot of time with diplomacy doing so. That was fair.

♦

It took less than an hour to pack everything up. I make sure I don't stick around after signing a contract. That provides the haunting mirage of renegotiation, and after burning my price into their pound of flesh, they would want to do that. The royal emissaries knocked on the front door as I slipped out a back window and scurried down the multifaceted boarding house wall. Before anyone had read the weird little disclaimers in the footnotes more than eight times, I was in the forest.

Sneaking through elvish forests is a matter of intensities. They were unenthusiastically looking for me, but I emphatically didn't want to be found. Had they mobilized everyone in the search, maybe—but they didn't. So they searched, and I slipped north, from crystal groves to jade, and into the deep woods the elves dwell upon like the sea.

Elvendom's jade forest was the Aethr'Le Mor Das'de Feyr Languid, the Eternal, Foam of the Green Sea's Depth, Ebon Pitch, what impatient humans called the

Languid Forest. It was carefully maintained chaos of unchecked old growth in geometric patterns. Elves didn't go to the Languid; they passed through. The Languid Forest served as a barrier between the intemperate sea, fickle with humans on top, and the crystal groves, the Aethr ro Dyus'My Tirryani'El Rosh'de Feyr Solange. I forget the translation, but humans called it the Solange.

The Solange was Elvenhome, where Their Majesties lived. Kings and Queens of Elvendom mostly dealt with each other, so the elves decided long ago that all their nobility should live in one place so they could have their very elegant bickering at their convenience. Every now and then, one went home to give someone the silent treatment, but doing so would result in that elvish noble withdrawing from politics on the whole. They can do it, but it reduces their power. It's rare, it's a statement, and that sword cuts the hand that draws it.

North of even the Languid are the deep woods, the Arsae. I approached via the Ridgeway, a spine of broken hills crested with flying arches, and could see the Arsae build. The highest canopy rose like mountains. Spires of trees formed white-capped peaks and scraped the hot summer sun as it passed, clad in the foamy thyf. It's easy to miss the road beginning to descend. I've come this way a few times, and each time I expect the crest to rise like foothills. It doesn't. The road begins to sink into the depression of Karas, and soon the final leap lands on the trunk of the Wayguard Sentinel and will touch land no more.

The deepest anyone I personally know has descended to measure the ground of the Karas was three thousand feet. It was a team of academics in Celephias, and they surveyed their way down and back. They believed the color of the surface mapped the depths of Karas, deeper ground inducing darker treetops, and estimated Karas's deepest pits were more than seven thousand feet below the Languid. The treetops there were more than ten thousand feet above the Languid. Decide your confidence in their estimates yourself.

From the Wayguard I found a cloud cutter and booked a cresting, the long haul across the Arsae to goblindom beyond. The captain was a creature of piano wire and overtightened springs, with knives for bones and sharp stones for eyes. He was elvish, and I would not want to meet him in a fight.

I said, "I'm looking for speed. Just me, over the crest to the goblin lands. Bloodharvest. I must be there before the weather changes. No other passengers, one bag"—I hefted my satchel—"no questions."

He looked me up and down. Somehow, I doubt he was eyeing my curves, but I bet he could count my knives from memory later. "*Regret* will take you there. You do know the crest, don't you? Speed comes at the cost of size. She's not thrice your height long."

"Speed above all," I said.

"*Regret* is fast," he repeated and nodded. "Mark over two. We sail—" He judged me. "Now."

I paid him, and he finally told me his name. Phillius, captain of the *Regret*, he was. My antipathy toward

9

inducing his hostility grew behind my eyes, but I paid him in fresh coins, human minted for Elvendom. They're worth slightly more than either human-for-human or elvish coins alone. Phillius took the two and pressed them. His sharp thumb bit the metal.

"We sail now," he affirmed.

Regret was flat and wide, an upturned table with four sails. She had no gunwales or cabin, just two low, long benches running from fore to aft. The masts weren't mated to the hull but to those benches. They would be weighted so she naturally stood on her heels, easing her toes above the thyf. Phillius told me where to sit, where to sleep, and to stay out of his way as he stowed my satchel out of mine. I accepted. One by one, danger signs went off in my head, but they didn't point the finger at Phillius. They waved in circles around him. I wanted badly to grab my intuition by the throat and scream 'Should I take this boat or not?' but she never answered that kind of question.

"I am ready," he stated.

Phillius was a dangerous machine. Elves aren't hard like that. They're natural. Sometimes they're powerful. They can be terrifying, and they hide unfathomable depths. Phillius wasn't a waiting flytrap; he was a wound clock full of knives. He shouldn't—

I paused. He looked exactly like—

"Do you know Jasper?" I asked.

Phillius ticked without a tock and looked at me.

"Aye. I sailed with him under Helen."

There was no need to ask if it was the same Jasper.

Dear God, they had sailed under Helen. Dear Lord of Mercy.

"I am ready," he repeated.

"Speed, Captain. Speed."

Phillius smiled, and I huddled by the benches.

◆

Regret caught a wind I barely felt, but saw in the rustle of thin branches and rippling leaves. She leaped before it. Phillius piled sail on the upwinds, driving our port and aft down. The ship's prow and starboard lifted as the wind kissed her. I worried she'd tip forward. If the edges caught, we'd be thrown. Little ships never carry safety belts, and this was thin thyf over hundreds, maybe thousands, of feet of canopy. Phillius didn't allow that to happen. *Regret* caught the wind clean, leaped forward, and then tried to skid to a stop for the next thousand miles.

He hung scoops up front and plows behind, the plows catching the wind low to rush forward and down. The scoops wanted to run forward and rise. They bellied upward. Both wanted to put us on our heels. Thyf grew like a carpet. I tapped it as it rushed by, and my finger kicked a wake of spores and minuscule blossoms, ghosts of water ferns, across the treetops. The leaves wrapped dark green borders around yellow stems. Four-masted *Regret* could run before any wind her captain had the desire, or madness, to chase. Phillius had sailed with Jasper under Helen. He kicked balancing stones from the scales of self-preservation and sped just to see the ripples they made.

At night, he stopped by what I can only assume was witchcraft, and we drew a slim privacy curtain between us. Cold air blew up from the forest below. Before sunrise he had the curtain down and sails ready, and when dawn blessed the world with heat, we were positioned to catch the wind differential and ride it to the strong hot winds of the day.

I asked him how he knew where to moor when we were five days out. Treetops delved into the sky like roots seeking water.

He judged me before answering. He always did. It inhibited questions.

"Whale-sign," he said after cold calculation.

We were cutting through a low-flying cloud, one that lay a hands-width above the Arsae and boiled before the wind. The cotton candy of spongy ferns, the reaching twigs of treetops, and the rushing steam made green waves. We kicked a wake behind us from where our aft broke the cloud, and cast a wake before us, where the fastest winds slipped under the sails, flowed over the broad deck, and threw cold spirals ahead like spikes.

Phillius pointed to a run of cloud geysers, where the fog seemed to erupt from the forest.

"Fresh. Out here, deep thyf will grow over that in a matter of days. There's a pod swimming below. When they breach, they break the forest cover. Wind blows across the confluence, and we moor by whale-sign to catch the gusts in the morning."

That was the longest thing he had ever said to me.

"Don't"—I paused—"things down below travel through whale-sign?"

"They do. The big ones, the ones that can't slip between spaces themselves. The lurkers, the grabbers, the snatchers. Some of the bigger spiders, the ones that hunt instead of spinning webs."

"They come up through whale-sign?" I repeated.

He looked irritated at having to repeat himself. "The grabbers. The snatchers. They come up at night. But the morning wind is strong."

That was the last night of the cresting I slept. At all.

♦

Winds rushed madly through the treetop peaks, angry that land life reached up to their high elements. They played evil games. Phillius knew their games, and sailed. He no longer slept by the sun, but by the play of wind and rain. We could go faster in the rain. Downhill we could outrun madness. Phillius tried.

Down the north side of the Arsae Crests, the tallest of the white thyfed treetops where the upper rains fell and drove us down toward the cloud floor below, we caught a harsh gale. It was a summer snowstorm, a furious mingling of winds. We ran like a sled, playing with the sails to check our speed. I was terrified. The prow wanted to catch and dig, and we raced across the treetops faster than horses. If the front end bit more than the subtle chamfer could deter, we would pitch and roll. The Celephians estimated the woods were thousands of feet deep here. Phillius grinned as cold sleet froze lightning-strike patterns in the wrinkles of his eyes. He put me in the back to lie beyond the rearmost edge, prone on an array of spars and straps above the spraying sleet of our wake. It was miserable, but we made such time

"Whales," he whispered, once only.

They breached, spun, and threw beads from their fins. In the gray monochrome of sleet and fog, black shadows ten times the size of our boat lanced like spears from the deep woods. White fin-tips cut clouds like their own nature. Then, smash! They crushed the thyf and dove, flat tails flicking. Maybe each rose once and maybe many times, but uncountable whales breached around us. Phillius swore they chased. His fingers twitched for a harpoon.

"Perhaps it's a game. 'Ware if they land on us," he whispered.

"What then?"

It was a stupid question, I know, but it slipped out.

Phillius's grin broke the ice on his face as it spread. "Bad luck."

◆

Faster than was reasonable, we made it to the northern edges of the Karas, where tall rock mountains broke the surface of wooded valleys. Thyf grew thick and wild, coarser than the fine cotton of the peaks. New trees shot leaves through the deeps, long dark crescents with white centers and black veins, or thick spades with harsh edges. Ghosthearts and jymlin, they were called.

Phillius sailed to a ridgeline he knew, a lightning bolt of interconnected peaks and cliffs that would lead beyond the depression to where the land was ground. He drifted to the very edge of stone and halted, *Regret* settling. White thyf capped the peak, but the air was hot and humid.

"The bad place is over that ridge," Phillius said.

The goblinmounts marched down to drown in the Arsae, and only their heads marked the end of the line. The crest Phillius indicated hung between condemned peaks. I could see their skulls before the trees took them, and behind us, nothing surfaced.

"Shall I leave you here?" asked Phillius, looking north.

Cautiously, I broke a small twig and licked it. Thin summer sap was turning bitter. We were very close to too late.

Very close was soon enough.

"Yes, but I'll need a ride back," I said.

"Do you know when?" he asked.

"No."

He thought about it.

"Good luck," he said, catching an eddy wind back toward the deeps. I had my satchel and my wits, and he was gone.

Arrival at Bloodharvest

I crossed the unpleasant rock before nightfall. Bald-headed mountains rose out of the trees, from cliffs, not beaches, and though thick waves of leaf and thyf beat against the stone, I had to be careful not to put a toe in. The cover might be thinner than it appeared, over forest deeper.

The easiest part was avoiding leaving tracks. The goblinmounts were bare of soil or dirt, just exposed rock, either gray or black. Some of the heads carried veins of marble, usually a black field with lines of yellow. The rock sizzled like it carried static. When I rounded the final crest, Bloodharvest rose before me, and the sun sank behind mountains on the horizon.

Goblins fear trees—and of the Arsae I understand— so they built their executioner prison where their mountains fight out into the forest sea. It looks like a fist. That's a violent gesture in goblindom, the raised fist. It represents the hit, and they wanted to make a statement. But elves don't come here. Whales avoid this place, and the elves sail the trees to hunt whales. (Most do. I wasn't sure about Phillius.) So Bloodharvest offended no one but the prisoners kept inside, and it was either an inward-seeking strike or one omnidirectional, punching the entire world.

I let night drown Bloodharvest. It remained only as a blot on the stars. I slept badly. Having hurried, I waited the next day. The sun beat moisture out of the trees, and down below the surface of the Arsae, a deeper ocean of fog fell out of sight. On the rock, the air felt thick enough to swim in. I sat, sweated, and waited. Phillius had made time beyond expectation. The second day passed like a flood, but on the third I heard thunder.

In the afternoon, a towering thunderhead rushed over the goblinmounts like a swarm of bugs. It beat the Arsae with lightning. From the cloud's top hung black banners, and each one showed an iron-tongued goblin with long fangs and red eyes. Goblins had woven lightning through the banners and released it from those iron tongues. From there it lashed the world. The cloud ran south toward Bloodharvest with banners rippling; dark banners on a dark cloud, and soon they fluttered before a dark sky. But I could see them until the lower mists hid the upper reaches of the cloud, spitting lightning from black tongues.

That cloud should have carried Throathurters. Their sigil was hands on a throat. These were new. Black-tongues, I guessed, but I wasn't familiar with them. I sloshed stale canteen water around my mouth. So be it. I wasn't sure how this was going to be a problem.

The storm came to Bloodharvest. The thunderhead choked out the stars before they could come to their glory and threw jagged lightning down to the prison.

Goblin hands on the Polyp grabbed the bolts and held them fast. So moored, the great storm cloud halted, and goblins started unloading their prisoners. Rain attacked the ground.

It's a treacherous traverse to the prison no matter what, and it's a nightmare in the wet dark. It's also the only time I could beat the watchers on the walls. They've laid the whole area with spy holes and hidden posts. If you're going to approach without Dread's army, you approach during a storm when the goblins are unloading their prisoners and the wardens are distracted. Otherwise you get spotted and die from a thousand poisoned arrows and darts. As it was, I approached across bare rock, cut to be slippery, over unseen cliffs maybe thousands of feet tall. The upper canopy of trees was invisible, save when lightning hit it. Then wind and rain made it a black mist.

I thought of Phillius, who stopped for the night near whale-sign. That's where hunting spiders climb; grabbers, snatchers, ones too big to move between trees without whale tunnels. The canopy was thin here. Something about that distracted me during my crossing.

Each mooring bolt of lightning jumped from the cloud and wove about the Polyp before being caught by goblin hands and remained for only a short while. Landside goblins worked hard to keep the cloud moored, and those skyside unloaded fast. Ozone stank. The thunderhead leaned forward, eager to be away from the terrible prison. They heaved goblins and packages from cloud to Polyp until a shout of "Loose!" echoed out. Goblin hands unleashed the lightning.

The thunderhead roared and fled Bloodharvest, charging out over the Arsae. I heard that sometimes the goblins can't steer back around to goblindom, and the storms rain fury and goblins over the Arsae until there's nothing left. I've just heard that. I've never seen it.

Rain pulled a thick mist from the peaks of the goblinmount, forming a nice avenue up to the broad base of the upper prison structure. Normally they're quick to get in after unloading, and the prisoners were already inside, but when I arrived two groups of goblin brass were loudly arguing with each other while lesser goblins tried very hard to be invisible. Tall goblins shouted at each other while staying within the bounds of Krat. Some of them were almost twice as tall as I with big heads, big eyes, and wet tusks sticking out of tooth-filled mouths. Sentries stared intently at the ground and the cloudy sky, but they didn't see me. It was almost like they weren't really searching, but listening hard to the fight behind them. I passed within inches of the outer sentries to get to a mooring pillar that was spiderwebbed with lightning burns and near the center of conversation.

"None of that matters if you can't meet your requirements!" yelled the leader of the newcomers, an immense Blacktongue. He was three meters tall and wiry. He looked like a beanstalk with a head.

"And the schedule means nothing now that the Artificer has left!" rebutted the Throathurter greeter. She wasn't quite as big, but her arms and legs were longer. Her fingers dangled, twitching, undulating. They wrapped around invisible necks and squeezed.

"You have an opinion, so clearly I don't want it," replied the newcomer.

"It is not a matter of opinion that the Artificer has left," snapped the Throathurter.

"Then it does not matter there, either."

The Throathurter seethed in quiet fury as Blacktongue guards waited. Long fingers danced on Throathurter hands, while Blacktongues smiled. Heavy goblin eyes shifted against each other.

Thirty or so Blacktongues formed a half ring around their leader. There were twice that number of Throathurters present. The newcomers commanded the center of the periapsis of the great prison, where the mountain had been flattened. Other than stray fronds of thyf, windblown up from the Arsae, the rock was barren. It would be a good place for a fight, and the Throathurters had numbers on their side. They had the Blacktongues surrounded.

Thirty Blacktongues waited. Their leader smiled cruel and cold.

The greeter submitted. "Come in. You may regard the labor and guide us."

"I may," repeated Blacktongue, amused, and his thirty nose-whistled at the Throathurter's generosity.

They marched in together, Throathurters falling in around and behind the newcomers without looking at them, and again no one spotted me. No one was looking for me, either; they were intent on not seeing each other at all. The Blacktongues pointedly didn't pay attention to anyone.

I followed. The goblin hegemony was a complex, incestuous, and fratricidal thing. The Throathurters had been ascendant as recently as a few years ago, but these Blacktongues bossed them about with clear disregard. I wasn't sure who they were. The Throathurters were mountain goblins, rife from the high peaks of the north to this, their furthest outpost in the ungoblined Arsae. Throughout their power plays, the Throathurters had maintained Bloodharvest since rebuilding it centuries ago. Back then, Whitehall had fallen into Kuranes the Seventh's trap. When Dread had laid siege to Bloodharvest, the goblin nations had known the prison was unconquerable if defended, and committed all their strength to it.

Some knowledge is just belief, and beliefs can be wrong. Dread had earned his name again. Whitehall was no more, and the tattered clans that survived never again united as one people.

◆

Once within the iron gates of Bloodharvest, I looked for an angry one, one with the light of hard cunning still in his eyes. Goblins will beat that out their underlings if they can. I spotted a brute who still had it, a hulking monster with sloped brows and lowered head who kept his eyes down. Goblins are bigger than humans, though, and I could look up and see banked hate in him. He looked around when no one was looking at him. He'd be perfect.

I followed him to his guard post, a darker shadow in dark-shadowed halls, and spied on him. The guards were tired, tense, and bored, and had no secrets. No one was sneaking toward the prison now, so they had nothing to talk about but each other. My target was named Lagganak, and he was not a Throathurter or a Blacktongue. He'd worked the storm clouds that goblins sail the Arsae, but had been injured and thrown away. Now he wasn't quite a prisoner, but he was here to die all the same. The other guards left to gossip about the new arrivals, and I whispered to him when he thought he was alone.

"Want to kill your boss?"

Lagganak—it meant 'bent hands'—startled. He manned an isolated guard post, far out under a distant arm of the Bloodharvest ridge. The window was marked with leaded glass inscribed with broken writing, Wardings that matched invisible spots on the stone. A squirrel skittered past one, a spider chasing it, and the Warding glass gleamed in savage red light. The light died as the running shadows vanished. There was no one else around. I stayed hidden as Lagganak searched for me.

"No," he said loudly, falsely, and suspiciously.

"Right, right," I agreed, equally false. "You wouldn't want that. But suppose you did?"

"No," he said again, softer. "I don't want to kill my boss and throw her corpse over the edge."

Jackpot. "Of course, of course," I agreed. "But suppose you did?"

Lagganak stopped trying to find me and looked out the small watch hole. Starlight fell on black trees. The sea was fair green by sunlight, but now it was the abyss.

"I'm loyal to Master Laptra," he said, and turned his back on me.

"What if I gave you a gift?" I suggested.

Lagganak looked up. This was so bizarre he didn't think it was a trap. I don't think goblins would think of gifts even as a trap. He knew the word, but it made no sense.

This was my last moment to change my mind, and I sized Lagganak up. Goblins don't have noses. Their nasal passages open into their mouths, and their large teeth prevent their lips from closing, even when they sleep. The mouth breathing makes it easy for humans to think them stupid, and this is not always wrong. But to think all goblins are stupid is a grave mistake, and to think them uncunning a mistake that ends in the grave.

Lagganak was smart, but tired, paranoid, and suspicious. The difficulties of his labors, continued into what should be a long shift, had sanded down the sharp edges of his head. That he looked clever anyway, skeptical of me and cynical of my offers of strange, shadow-bound gifts in the middle of the night, indicated that wide awake, he would be quite a problem. My head was chest high on him, and in the way of goblins, he was lean. His hands were very quick. He had long arms, long legs, and a wide upper body that looked flatter than humans' round torsos. His shoulders bowed from the high crest of his short neck to low joints. His fingers were bent, as his name suggested, but they should be able to hold a sword.

By odd convenience, I had one for him.

"I have here the Departing. You know this blade. It was made for the old Fiefdom Wars. Whitehall goblins caught lightning when the Great Winter came, winter so cold lightning froze out of the sky and fell like lead. They smithed those lightning bolts into swords when the cold burned like fire. This is a goblin sword for the slaying of goblins."

While I talked, I opened a black felt bundle I had carried and exposed a white blade. A remnant of starlight leaked through the window and set it dancing. Lagganak hissed as he sucked his teeth. The Departing glittered.

"Melbrod," he whispered.

"I have heard it called that."

I exposed more of the blade, down to the handle where a broad, black gem was set at the conflict of handle and edge. The gem caught no light even as the blade above amplified it.

Lagganak's eyes were wide as mouths and deep as ambition.

To seal the deal, I lifted a scrap of firepaper, scratched it, and let it burn down to my fingers. His eyes said I had him now. The firepaper crackled, and the blade danced. Fire reflected sharper than the blade edges, and that reflection paid no attention to straight or vertical, lunging and leaping like combat beyond where the blade should be. It looked a bit like lightning in my fist. The gem reflected nothing. It stayed cold, dark, and hard, like Lagganak's lust-filled eyes.

He didn't lust for me. I smiled.

The firepaper winked out, and I danced aside to other shadows in the sudden dark. I laid the Departing down and let it scrape the stone.

"Here. A gift," I whispered from yet another shadow.

"A gift," I echoed.

"A gift," the night echoed, for I was gone.

I gave four more gifts by sunrise, and by then I needed some sleep. I had no more gifts. No one had started murdering their bosses yet, and wouldn't until sunset. Goblins who don't sleep during the day tend to brood. They might not start murdering their bosses come nightfall, either. Those who maintained their independence did so by turning inward. They might be more used to hiding their hate than using it, even with the swords of goblin killing I'd given them. I would have to do something about that. Later, I decided.

I curled up in a clutter closet and slept, dreaming of luxuries like a bed, covers, and the absence of whatever this stupid rock thing in my back was. I swear it followed me when I moved.

At nightfall I awoke, somewhat rested. I ate from my bag, drank canteen water, and sat out a changing of detail. Goblins trudged from position to position. Some warded the prisoners, some made hoops in iron foundries, and others carried out a dozen small jobs of the executioner fortress. I went looking for the prince. This would be a monumental waste if he was already dead.

♦

Another thing about goblins is that they don't see contrast well. In the dark, they can see better than humans, perhaps even better than elves, but a torch washes it out so they see only the fire and shadowy blurs. In sunlight they can see fine, perhaps not as well as humans but functionally. They can't see into deep shadows from broad daylight. A goblin would be blind looking from sunlight into a cave or vice versa. They can't see in pitch black, and in the deepest places of Bloodharvest, what they call the True Dark, they have difficulty even with lanterns. That worries me.

Thus, their construction aims for an allover dim. When they build, they rarely build light fixtures, and those they do are heavily shrouded. Their lanterns use more quartz than glass. When they use torches at all, they ring them in iron shades to throw the light against the ceiling. It's a pragmatic decision since they see best in bright light or gloom, and gloom is easier. One has to work to keep a building bright. Gloom comes on its own.

For a few buildings, their builders went the other way, and those goblins revel in illumination that puts human palaces to shame. The Temple of Luminance is magnificence, sunrise recreated in marble and oil. I've been there once but didn't get to appreciate it. (Someone was trying to stab me.)

When sneaking around Bloodharvest, I would find the brightest light source I could and skirt it. I stayed five steps from torch light cones and haunted corridors that led to bonfires. The zone where torchlight falls from bright cone to caster of shadows was my demesne. Inside the mammoth prison, steel gates separated the sections but always hung open. The cells were always closed. I spied on their kitchens for hours, hidden in pockets of fireplace dark and listening to the cooks argue in thick goblin pidgin about which prisoners would get food today. The jailers stood close enough that I considered tapping them to prove I could.

The cooks were mostly Bloodharvest lifers, goblin prisoners who would never leave and worked for the wardens in exchange for comfort. They spoke a prison dialect I didn't know and ostensibly refused to understand the guards. Their wardens were all southern Throathurters.

In practice, enough jailers knew the prisoner dialect and vice versa to make themselves understood, with brute violence layered on top like pond scum over the deeps. The violence wasn't unnecessary to them. Many of their deliberate communication errors seemed to have no purpose but to elicit it.

I found someone who grunted of 'karashak,' 'Arsae sailors' in Throathurter. He was an old, twisted goblin who carried buckets of cold-pressed bread from the kitchens to the cells with discretion over who ate that day. When he mentioned karashak, I shadowed him from the kitchen, skirting light and darkness. He looked over his shoulder twice and didn't see me. By the time we got to the elven cells, he was talking to himself about Bloodharvest getting to him.

Two elves took the food ration at a many-occupant cell. Some were chained to the walls, while others were free. Whether or not the wall-bound prisoners ate was a decision for their comrades. The Throathurter taunted them as they fed those on the walls, for all of them were starving. Soft mutters passed from elf to elf.

Once the prisoner waiter was gone, I tapped softly on the barred door and whispered in Elvish, "Hello."

The entire cell went dead silent.

"Peace." I whispered again. "I am Astrologamage Elegy. I am from the Solange. Is Prince Aehr among you?"

That was a silence of horror. Grumbles and clicks from distant cells sounded through the bedrock, and the weight of metal on closely laid blocks creaked. It was so quiet I could hear pulses throbbing in elvish necks, the beat of skin on metal in the poor waifs manacled to the walls.

One of them appeared. Trees grow faster than that elf edged into the light of the doorway, moving from deep shadow to what would be deepest shadow anywhere else. His tall eyes rose like dovetails from his thin nose, and his skin hung from him. His face wasn't even monochrome, but wet with varying shades of black.

"He may be known to me," whispered the elf.

"Well for his sake I hope he is, because I've been paid to get him."

Something broke in that elf. Some inner reserve of pride, a hint of hope.

"He won't leave without everyone." His voice tasted of the poison of despair.

The other elves did not do the same. A many-throated ghostly sigh escaped them, as if everyone else in the cell suddenly put down a burden.

"That's not necessary," whispered someone else in High Elvish. The voice had problems making click sounds because part of her tongue was missing. "We do not need freedom"—she said with terrible longing—"if we know we have protected you."

"Everyone comes," snapped Aehr. "Or I die here too!"

I used some humanisms.

Elves are aware of swearing even if they don't do it. Being rude, it's something they ignore. While humans might ignore profanity in anger, to elves it's rain over the ocean. Half-tongue's argument and Aehr's refusal were far more important to them than my muttering.

"How many others is everyone?" I asked when we were done.

"Forty-three," said the prince.

"Forty-three?" asked one of the others, accenting the three, and the prince hissed in reply. "He helped us. He comes!"

I tried to look past the prince to get a sense of the others, but they stayed submerged in the darkness of the cell. Even Aehr was wet with shadow. Around few corners up a hallway, a fire burned, but the amber firelight splashed off so many walls, it was almost nothing when it got here. Part of the ceiling was obsidian, illuminating Aehr from above so shadows dripped from his nose and the sharp edges of his eyebrows. I wouldn't have been able to see him at all if I'd seen daylight within the last day.

"So forty-four elves total?" I asked. "Including you?"

"Forty-three elves and one goblin," said the prince.

I used more humanisms.

My initial plan—start a fight, sneak out, shank everyone who gets in my way—wasn't going to work. Not for forty-four. I sat in the darkness and thought. Elves are patient. They didn't intrude.

"How many can walk?" I said, finally.

"We'll carry those who can't," whispered the prince.

"Yes, I know, but I'm thinking about speed."

There was a long silence; it was my turn to wait. Feet shuffled in the cell, movement done with such silence that their breathing might have been louder. Prince Aehr returned with the count. "Twenty-eight can walk. Twelve can limp. Three or four must be carried."

This was going to be a nightmare.

"Are you at least all together?" I demanded.

"No. There is one who is not here."

I winced. Several other elves hissed at their prince.

"He goes with us!" he snapped inward, to others in the cell. He was furious with despair.

"Tell me where he is so I can get him," I grumbled. This was not in my contract, but I wouldn't build my name by half-assing the job.

They gave me directions, and I told them to prepare. For what, I didn't know, but those immobile should have their limbs chafed and those who could walk should be prepared to carry the rest. I didn't know how. I didn't know when. I knew why—money—but the means to that end escaped me like the prisoners hadn't. I nodded to myself.

"Do you ever leave your cells?"

"Yes. Those who want to eat must delve mines. They will come for us at sunset and task us until dawn. It is our only clock."

How long had I been creeping around? I needed more sleep.

"Prepare as you can," I whispered, and left.

Before the True Dark

slept, ate, stole rainwater from a cistern, and went hunting Aehr's goblin.

Along the way, I spotted Lagganak in a meal line. The goblin before him was being berated for moving too quickly between a senior and a cook fire. That goblin, Thotic, was filthy, worthless, and fit for death. Lagganak said nothing. The bent-handed one kept his eyes down, but his expression was peculiarly judging. He weighed the yelling Throathurter from the corners of downcast eyes.

In a warren of goblins, a hidden one was hard to find. There was more freedom at sunrise and sunset, while the light was changing. Most of the cells were in the fist of Bloodharvest, the body of the Polyp that grew on a fat stem of rock above the goblinmount. During movement to the tunnels, the prisoners and guards saw traces of sun. Even down below, guards with their lanterns brought a shifting twilight to the tunnels. This was when the braziers and torches were replenished, changing the shoals of gloom between the islands of light and deep shadows. The jailers moved slowly, and if they moved prisoners, they would frequently stop them for mild excuses at the borders of light and dark. Deeper underground, Bloodharvest stabilized into perpetual gloom. In the eternal dark, goblin eyes worked better than mine. I spent hours hiding from nothing. Often, I heard noises I could not recognize and froze in the grimmest holes on the chance a guard waited up ahead. When one didn't, I wanted to barge on carelessly, but I refused, staying safe, and crept forward to outwait the next creaking wooden plank.

Old, dry wood flexes on its own, sometimes. It sounds exactly like a muffled footstep. I learned the floorboards by name.

Othrak, the goblin I hunted, was kept in an airborne cage, a bird's nest too small for a human and terrible for a long-limbed goblin. It hung in still air from an old chain. I arrived at feeding time, and a guard was taunting him with a pot of stew.

Othrak looked exhausted, hungry, and defeated.

When the guard could not elicit a reaction, he threw the stew at the prisoner. Some of it splashed through the bars and some fell. The guard laughed and left. Othrak wiped grain meal from himself and his cage, and ate it.

There was no one around. I waited. Othrak's cage hung from a chain, lowered through a shaft where dim lights formed a gray column. Below there were echoes of wind in deep places. I scoured the nearby enclosures and confirmed there were no guards, so stepped onto the catwalk, tapped my foot twice to alert Othrak of my presence, and strode out to speak with him.

"Hello, Othrak," I said in Elvish.

He was so weary he did not look surprised, but merely rolled his head upright. He stared at me for a while, letting shadow resolve into figure. He could see I wasn't goblin before his mind recalled I'd spoken something else. Each tired breath shook his lips.

"Who?" he asked.

"Elegy. I'm here for Prince Aehr. He remembered you."

Othrak stared at me. He squinted and widened his eyes, stretching tired muscles. I don't think he'd had anything to look at in a long time, for the motion seemed unfamiliar.

"You—who?"

"Elegy. Prince Aehr remembers you."

"One is—remembered?"

"You are."

I looked around. This was the situation humanisms were invented for.

Othrak's cage was ten feet from the closest catwalk, and his feet hung at eye level. Even if I made the jump, I would have to catch one of his limbs, and his dirty skin would be slippery. Malnourished as he was, the shock would probably break his joints. That wouldn't work. I'd have to find the top of the chain and descend, which meant I needed rope. A malnourished goblin weighed as much as I did or more, so I didn't know how I was going to accomplish this.

The pit below descended indefinitely. Other rooms like this one opened from the sides of the cavernous drop, and I could see no bottom. When I dropped a stone, it fell in silence. If there were echoes, the wind ate them. Above, the shaft climbed through the stem of the great prison into the fist of Bloodharvest.

I looked back to Othrak.

"Tell Prince Aehr I remember him," said Othrak.

"I will. How are you caged? Is there a lock?"

Othrak responded with defeated silence, and I pressed him twice more for an answer.

"There is no lock. It's riveted."

Oh, goodness.

Othrak spoke slowly. "One is never freed from the Blackdrop. One is shackled and left, until the guards forget to feed the one. When no one remembers the prisoner's remains, the one is gone."

I stared at him in silence. That was four, five hundred pounds of iron cage plus chain. I was going to need a winch or a block and tackle. I thought of the goblin.

"You are not forgotten. Prince Aehr recalls you."

"The soul lives on the lips that speak a name. I will enjoy living in elvish sunlight."

No, that's not the way this ends, I decided, and circled the chamber again.

Two other chains descended through the light pillar. They hung passive, iron links woven with some thick cord. I stared at them, thinking. They didn't vibrate. A hint of wind blew up from the abyss. I had to look for a while before that made an impression. The chains didn't vibrate at all.

"Othrak, can you wiggle a little? Will the cage swing?"

He faintly shook a toe. The cage jiggled and swung. In time it stilled, but for a while it arced. I threw pebbles at the other chains. They swung, but their vibrations died quickly. Something down below had to be anchoring these chains.

"Othrak, how deep does this go?"

"To the Well of Memory."

"Is that a place, or are you speaking—"

"Tell Aehr I remember him," said Othrak, and lay back against the bars.

His arms and legs stuck from the birdcage akimbo, and his head slumped. Only faint movement of his lips betrayed his breathing.

I started thinking in angles. Forty-three elves could—might be able to lift an iron cage with a thin goblin. How much iron chain? The cage was riveted, not locked. If it was swung to the side, it would have to be held in place. It would be above the catwalk. A holding structure would be built, while the rivets—the catwalk would not hold. The cage must be lifted to the next level and pulled aside. The catwalk shook under my light foot. It wouldn't hold. Some mechanism had to exist to lower the cage. Down was away from escape. I thought and I thought.

◆

I went up to a guard house high in the Polyp, where many goblins laughed. In a common area, a single lamp cast gloom while the guards threw bones and argued about who they would stab. An inner room had a door wedged open and a veil of shadows that exhaled cold wind. The air was dead of scent, but it whispered. This should be about the right place.

I eased past when an argument about politics reached violent extremes and found a room with three winches mounted to an iron grate. The grate capped a circular hole in the floor with iron rings, each one inside an off-center larger ring. An outer diameter ring was threaded into the stone. A single hole in the center of the grate was as big as my leg, but the winches fed chain through their undersides where they were bolted down. My arms couldn't reach the played-out end under the grate, and of the three winches, two were completely played out. The drum body of the other was encased in an iron shield. I couldn't even see the chain.

Turning to the shielded gears, I discovered Othrak's winch had been rendered unable to roll up. It only unrolled down.

Why? I asked myself. Goblins, I answered.

Could it be rolled up anyway? Certainly. A blacksmith could break the one-way locks with ease if he hadn't been chained to a wall in goblin prison until he could no longer walk. If he had tools. If a horde of goblins wouldn't investigate the noise. If we had warriors to fight them off instead of enfeebled elves.

I was no blacksmith. The file I'd brought for manacles was meant to be hidden between the fingers or in a shoe. I took it out and stared at the monstrous metal work, an iron spool bigger than I was. Those fantasy warriors had better be able to hold off the goblin hordes for a while.

If necessary, I bet the elves would try. They'd try and die.

Twice I had spoken to the elves, so they knew I had not left. Aehr's estimation of how many could walk was hopelessly optimistic. Standing and moving from one end of a narrow cell to the other was not walking through miles of tunnels. To where? There was no boat.

I descended, wondering where Othrak's cage would land. Of course, goblins don't build for safety, and occasionally limitless chasms opened up with no warning. A hurried step where the weight was committed before the floor was found and a bit of Phillius's 'bad luck,' and everyone would die alone. It kept me on my toes.

The Meeting Below

This was the third time I'd come to, or near, Bloodharvest. The first time, I had been farther north at the Temple of Luminance, and there had been a bit of confusion, some hostility. I might have thrown someone out a window, and his nephew might have chased me. I may have thrown a burning lantern at the nephew and possibly insulted his goblinhood while he danced in flames. He had been unhappy with me for something. The details are fuzzy.

For whatever reason, I'd left the Temple with great haste, stowed away on a storm cloud, and ridden it to Bloodharvest. I hadn't gone in, but disembarked, spied, and climbed away across the goblinmounts back north. It had been a bad trip. With stealth, endurance, and starvation, I'd made it back to human lands.

The second time had been more deliberate. A figure in a yellow cloak had met me under cover of night, piled money on my lap until I asked no questions, and ordered me to return to Bloodharvest. My mission was to sneak in and liberate someone from the cells. That someone had been Luthas, a gaunt man without a face. Plain skin had stretched from his chin to eyebrows, and when he talked, the shape of lips and a nose would press forward against the mask like a child playing behind a wet cloth. Luthas had been held in the lower reaches of the prison, in caverns forgotten by goblins. They don't go down there. There are terrible things down there, things like Luthas, and goblins are not stupid. I had liberated him from thick chains, worn down by age.

The stranger had given me a sign to show the other things that haunted the lower reaches. They had left me alone, though as long as I remained beneath Bloodharvest they followed outside the bubble of my lantern. They waited and watched from the darkness. I wrote the sign on all four panes of my lantern, a good human lantern with clear glass, but it cast so many shadows.

Luthas had not cast a shadow. I remember that keenly. I like to tell myself it was because the hole was dark and the stone was black, but that's a lie. After watching the figures outside the light watch me, I knew every shadow by name. I could find a shadow cast from Pallas up between stars. Luthas cast no shadow. He'd thanked me and crept away, heading down. I'd spoken to him no more.

♦

There was no way to reel Othrak up. Every plan had fatal errors. But it wasn't that hard to lower him, and I could do that alone. All I needed was a distraction to get the goblins out of the room next to the winches. One could be arranged. I needed to find out where the bottom of the Well of Memory was, though, so down I went. If it went into Luthas's True Dark, I'd kept the lantern that had granted me safe passage before and remembered the stranger's directions. I'd rather risk myself and one other to stealth than all of us and my money ticket to a fight.

I went down. It was long and unpleasant. I prefer not to think about it. The dark was relentless with iron gates sealed against it. Nothing moved. For days I searched, until during endless rounds of checking and rechecking, I found a gate unbarred. You can imagine my surprise when I approached what should be the bottom of the well and found a broad ring of Blacktongues holding high lanterns. Each of the thirty tall goblins wore yellow robes. They stared out into the encroaching darkness with the color of fear, but their arms never wavered. They carried lanterns of a sort I've never seen in goblin hands before. Each had one glass pane, etched with a coarse script I didn't recognize. The light they cast was too bright for goblin eyes in the deeps, but the shadow of the etched writing lay bold on the walls. Even to human eyes, the shadows were thick among the lanterns. They smeared the goblins and splattered their robes. It was easy to hide among them. I flitted through the high contrast between goblins of the circle and noticed pieces of iron on the ground. Spars of rusty metal lay in patterns I didn't have the perspective to understand.

The two at the center carried out an old argument, one beyond the point of conclusion that had distilled to restatement of positions. Rumor had named the Blacktongue

Thern, and Lagganak had called the Throathurter Laptra. She was something between warden and high priestess of Bloodharvest. The Blacktongues followed Thern, but I didn't know his position.

My position was behind him and a little to his right. He'd hooked his yellow robes behind a sword on his belt, some unnamed steel that still gleamed. I crouched within the goblin line by a pile of fallen ceiling stones. They provided hardly any cover, but in my work clothes, with goblins carrying peculiarly un-goblinish lights behind me, I was a small fish in the Fhysay.

"Drop the one," said Thern. "Feed the Hungry Silence."

Laptra inhaled and shut her lips over her fangs. She moistened her teeth and swallowed.

"We talked about this," she said, clenching her jaw so upper and lower fangs ground against each other as she spoke. "It's too early. Fame carries the one's name throughout the bones of Whitehall. When the darkness eats, they want a rich, thick meal, whispered on a thousand goblin tongues in shadows, spoken in back rooms and alleys, and asked of silence itself. The longer we let the one marinate, the greater the feast—"

"I don't care about that one," interrupted Thern. Laptra sucked air, held it, didn't speak. Thern continued. "There are old powers down here, and they will pay in knowledge for names. The one is a thin price no matter how widely spread. Put the elves in the Blackdrop, and I will buy the wisdom of shadows when they eat."

"But we cannot put the prince in the cages until the last morsel is dropped. We did that to kill hope—"

"So kill the one!" yelled Thern, interrupting her again. "The princeling's name is spoken by karashak whalers. Old powers promised—"

"Old powers promise and do not pay!" interrupted Laptra.

Thern shouted her down. "Old powers are quick to pay! They have the wealth of ages, and it means nothing to them. I have seen fountains of money! Drop the one, then cast the princeling and two to the Blackdrop. The Hungry Silence will smell them, taste them, hear them whisper to each other between their cages. Hunger will drive the silence mad! The old powers will pay knowledge for flesh."

He looked at her oddly. "Why do you argue when you win with me? Now you are locked here, with only one storm anvil a year. The old powers will teach us ways around that! They will teach us why the Karas depths eat weather, save the twilight of summer. That is what we bargained for with the Artificer, and he escaped! Kill the one, kill the elves, and the people will sail south over the Arsae when the whalers think they are safe. Lightning burns their trees while little birds hide inside. Bloodharvest may become its name, the fist thrown against karashak." His breath smelled almost, but not quite, like blood.

Laptra banked her hate. Her eyes glittered with it, but she looked down as Lagganak had. While Thern shouted at her and his Blacktongues laughed, she endured. When he was done, she continued as if he had not spoken, but stress showed in the way she slipped.

She said, "The one committed crimes for karashak no goblin will ever forget. He stood against Krat when it was one goblin and one elf. His fame will live on tongues forever. When his cage finishes the Blackdrop we will throw bells from the wellmouth. Their chiming gathers the Hungry Silence, but the sharks of deep stillness are both attracted to and repelled by noise. The bells fall ringing into water, and the churn throws them up. The Hungry Silence waits. Eventually, by chance, the bells will be silent long enough for one of the shades to get through. Arms and legs stick outside the cage. They nibble. The rootwater throws a bell up, and they flee. They wait. The cage will be silent before the last bell rings." Laptra looked inward.

Thern whispered. "I tell you something, you do not listen, you then speak against a point I never made."

Laptra ignored him. "The name of the one in Blackdrop is flourishing. The name grows fat. In six months or a year when the one is dropped, the Hungry Silence shall feast. But first he must suffer. He must hurt."

Thern turned away from her. The larger goblin hurled a stone into a bubbly pool. The rock splashed through the froth and sank, but moments later surfaced. A ripple caught it, slung it into another, and the small rock hopped from the water. It remembered to fall several yards up and splashed back down. The froth juggled it. For the first time, I noticed the pool fed a sluice gate on the far side of us, but the stream from that gate rushed uphill. It stayed neat in its channel, save the bubbles and spray as it tumbled up and away. Two empty cages hung peculiarly still a few feet above the water. Water from the Blackdrop pool murmured as it fell uphill.

"Bloodharvest is the hole of suffering," Laptra was saying.

"Think of what we could do with that water in our storm anvils," whispered Thern.

"And we will let him marinate," said Laptra. "You argued when I took the time to teach him fame is all important. It was me who told him treachery for the elves would make him immortal. From the beginning, you have acted impatient as a shelling."

Thern looked up, his eyes wide. Wrapped up in her narrative and turned inward, Laptra missed the goblin ring start to chuckle.

She continued. "Yes, I wasted time courting the Artificer's vanity. He thought he was a power of the flesh, but what he really wanted was praise. How long had he made a nest by the rootwater in the darkness without us knowing, and how did he escape without going up? But this time, we will be smart. We will wait and drop the one—"

"You who are weak, how much do you think your life matters?" asked Thern. "How much do you think my masters care if you live or die?"

The Blacktongues hissed. Laptra shot glances at him and all thirty of the others. I didn't believe it. Thern had waited for Laptra to speak first, and it had slipped out of her, I'm sure. She hadn't noticed calling him a shelling. It was just a thought that eased between her teeth into words. But he had responded in kind.

They weren't really thinking of invoking Krat down here. There were thirty of them to hold the silence at bay. They didn't mean—

Into Laptra's stunned silence, Thern spoke. "Correct. That much."

"Thern—"

"No weakness. No denial. Do it, or I will kill you."

The goblin circle hissed, and tall lanterns wavered. They listened hard. Only violence or submission could follow Thern's demand, and the goblin rules of etiquette, Krat, bound Laptra to fight if she wouldn't submit. The thirty goblins outside listened. If she won, they would come to kill her one by one. Krat was not about being fair.

"Thern—" said Laptra.

Thern smiled, and his thick, black tongue seethed. I smelled something weird, like hot metal. I wasn't sure what.

Laptra didn't finish, and our island of light was still. Immense pressures bore against her on all sides.

"It will be as you say," she said.

The thirty outside did not relax, but inched fractionally about to look to Thern. They waited.

The great Blacktongue smiled. His teeth were long and filthy.

That blood smell was iron. His breath smelled like hot iron.

"You submit because you are weak," Thern added.

Laptra looked like she was desperate for anything, but there was nothing. She forced herself to wilt.

"Yes," she said.

We all heard it. Her shoulders slumped, her back bent, and she bowed to him.

"And for being weak, you will die."

Her head snapped up as Thern threw his head back and screamed. Chains and horror erupted instead of sound.

He shrieked steel bangles. Thick iron links leaped from the dark pit of his jowls and lashed at Laptra. Instead of a tongue, chains sprayed toward her. She leaped aside, and her hands flashed for his neck. In an instant, she caught him and he caught her, and iron and iron-fingers ground against different fleshes.

The ring of thirty lowered their lanterns and looked between themselves, several making soft whimpering sounds. A few shuffled their feet.

"She was to refuse," one whispered, agitated.

"This was always the plan," another hissed.

"But the plan was she would refuse?" The first turned it to a question.

"It doesn't matter."

"It is Krat!" screamed Laptra, even as iron cut her skin.

The goblins outside hemmed and shuffled their feet, and a few hissed so thin chains of rusty iron slithered from their lips. Baby cobras of reddish steel hovered, but the thirty did not move. Laptra squeezed Thern's neck as his iron gouged her flesh. Chain caught her neck and tried to pull the Throathurter's arms away. She squeezed. Laptra's hands began to shake, but Thern's throat endured. Metal links pulsed where his airway should be.

Well, all things considered, I opened Thern's kidneys from behind.

I plunged a finger-sized blade in and out five times between his right side and spine, grinding like I'd hit bone every stab. Thern was so thin it was easy to forget he was ten feet tall, and I had to reach up to get over his belt. Laptra's fingers distracted him, and he didn't even notice until I had thrown myself away and down, crouching below eye level for the yellow-robed Blacktongues, giants themselves, and Laptra and Thern's immense struggle. Then, suddenly, Thern buckled sideways, his body curling toward his injured side, and the chains broke at his lips, parting like threads of spit.

Laptra screamed, "You are all betrayers of Krat!"

The robed guards sprang into action, shrieking chains of their own, and iron lanced toward her. She had a plan. From a hidden pocket, she grabbed a fistful of metal and hurled tiny and silver somethings to the floor before diving into the foaming pool at the heart of the Well of Memory. Bells bounced off the floor and rang.

The somethings bounced once. Half of them chimed again. A few rang a third time as Blacktongue chains dove into and through the foam-covered water. The guards had lowered their lanterns. Some had dropped the lights, and the shadow runes written on the chamber walls were distant and broken. Fewer bells chimed again, and then no more. They rolled, tinkling, across the stone for an instant, and I screamed:

"Lift the lanterns, FOOLS!"

War borne instincts were fast. The shadows rushed in as yellow arms lifted iron lanterns, and only a few were snatched by the Hungry Silence and vanished. Iron fell and banged. The lanterns wavered.

Outside the shadows reached. Dense, full shadows that radiated presence. Not the shadows of a dark house that might hide someone and might not. These had no uncertainty. The shadows twisted and reached as the Blacktongues tightened their circle. The lanterns lifted high, throwing a harsh wall against the night.

Elsewhere, in the water, Laptra's head crossed the surface as she swam uphill. Her form vanished through the sluice gate.

I had just given away the element of surprise after stabbing the Blacktongue leader, and the Hungry Silence had found us.

Humans have so many great words for situations like this.

♦

As I crouched, the goblins held back the Silence. Their lanterns were a wall against the shadows. Thern lifted himself on one arm, trying to get upright.

No one had spotted me yet, but they would. The circle divided their attention between the twitching shadows and searching for me, with Thern distracted by the stabbing and bleeding. I gained nothing by being found. I might gain awe with a reveal.

"Lift your lanterns!" I yelled, and stood up, stepping forward and flapping my cloak so it crackled and boomed. "Stamp your feet! Shout and cry! Silence against the dark is only useful as stealth. You have been found! Now fight with noise and power!"

I shovel-kicked some bells, sending a chiming wave of silver skittering across the floor. The shadows reared up but could not advance.

Attention on me, Thern yelled, "Who is that?"

"I am Maru Ghostheart. I was Dread's concubine, betrayed outside the walls of Bloodharvest. He sent me to the gates to negotiate, knowing Whitehall would meet me. They did, but my lover raked us all with arrows. My lover could not even lay me down in dignity, but had my body thrown to the Arsae," I said.

Thern hissed. He looked suspicious. The goblin wall doubted.

The Hungry Silence beat against the wall of lanterns, and the goblins hopped and danced lest a shadow grab a foot. Something black and terrible flowed up the walls. The incomplete runes, written on glass and cast in shadow, acted as a dam, but the dark probed for a way. It was possible the Hungry Silence could get around the lanterns from above. I bet that would be bad.

By Krat, Thern could insult and try to kill me, but he asked, "Can you get us out?"

"Yes," I replied. "But all the lanterns must be lifted. And you must sing."

Finally, Thern acted. "Lift the lanterns! Sing of Whitehall and the goblin nation that was lost!"

Blacktongues sprang to obey.

Traitors sang bravely. As they pushed to the fallen lanterns and swept the leering shadows away with light, they sang. Without command, they found a three-part harmony, something like a fugue divided by tone as well as repetition. The bass singers lead, the tenors followed, and the altos chased, but they all trod on the same beat. The Silence drew back.

Whitehall stood in goblin blood,
Its bones were tall and proud
It had no nails
Fellfinger fists
Held skinny roof to ground

Evil Dread of Kuranes dead
Marched like fire from the sea
Glory days to tree-burner way
Whitehall broke the advancing tree

An island in the enemy fist
We broke his fingers
pulled his nails
Long white teeth sank to bone
to deny the Heart Traitor
a Whitehall throne

Bled dry on rock
His cruel growth stopped
Dread went no further than the sea
His roots we killed
Whitehall drilled
A heart tap to save the free

They tell it a bit differently in Celephias.

Goblins have big lungs and deep voices, and the fugue allowed them to breath without letting the song pause.

The Hungry Silence gathered but could not advance. With all the lanterns raised and yellow-robed goblins making a firm wall, we marched away. I took a few fist-fuls of bells but wrapped them in a bit of felt so they could not sing.

Thern bled from his side. Most of the blood was deep red, but some was black. It smelled like bile and rust. I'd hit his liver, and as he lost blood, his skin shrank. I could see every muscle on him, the veins and tendons, and chain running through his flesh like a metal circula-tory system. He ignored it and commanded his Black-tongues with strong words. The party marched upward, ever singing, with tall Thern calling the turns. A wall of shadow followed.

Soon, perhaps a few eons later, we came to a wall of iron with cunning gates. The latches were all inside. Thern stuck his wiry arm through a hole and caught a cold-iron latch. The metal door swung inward. He marched his singing Blacktongues through and slammed the door shut behind.

Finished, he fell down dead. Outside the metal, the Silence waited. I fulfilled my claimed identity and ghosted away.

♦

I found an unoccupied bit of shadow in the upper reaches of the tunnels beneath the Polyp and sat down, staring at a wall. I felt blank. That was a little outside the usual goblin repertoire, and I just breathed for a while. It was safe enough to light my lantern and watch the shadows of my fingers make ducks. They were cute, safe, and empty.

It wasn't just things like Luthas, but the darkness itself. I'd been walking through darkness for days without a light, and the Hungry Silence was in here with me. I had to get Aehr, forty-two elves, and a goblin out of here. I had to stay hidden. There were things in the dark. The Blacktongues were something different, something worse. I had to free Aehr.

I didn't even know what the prince looked like. He was just an elvish voice in in the shadows.

I had to get moving.

I found Lagganak in his rooms, and said hello like this: "Bent Hands, greetings. Elegy, Gift Giver, Sword Bearer, greets you. Laptra submitted to Thern's will, and he attacked her. He has violated Krat."

"She's dead?" he whispered.

I considered my answer. It was a dramatic pause.

"Yes. She's dead."

"She must have challenged him. The Blacktongues, she challenged them all."

"No," I said. "Thern has violated Krat. She submitted, and after that she died."

"No Blacktongue would violate Krat."

"He has—"

"I don't believe you!"

The Departing crackled to his grip, leaping from scabbard to swing with the sizzle of thunder. His speed was blinding.

So was the darkness, and I had never revealed myself. He laid the sword against the stone wall, and

Bloodharvest thundered. Brilliant sparks tore apart the air. The stone quaked. For an instant, I was lit, plain as day, crouched by a meat sack.

"Liar!" screamed Lagganak, and swung thunder again.

He wasn't even close. With goblin vision washed out by lightning in a dark room, he might as well have been blindfolded. After the first slash, I'd rolled. I had covered one eye, the other open and now blind, but switched so I could see him flailing around where I had been. Now I closed my useless eye and ran.

Barely any distance up the hallway, I saw the first of the others, goblins come running to see why a thunderstorm crashed and banged inside. I was covered by brilliant light and shadows from behind. They raced past shouting, and Lagganak shouted back.

"Where is Laptra? Have they killed her, Thotic?"

"Probably," said Thotic. "Thern of Blacktongue is dead, so they killed each other by Krat."

"Do you know or do you speculate? Do you know they obeyed Krat?" yelled Lagganak.

Another goblin, I didn't catch his name, argued, "What do you mean, 'obeyed Krat?' It is Krat!"

"Do you know?" demanded Lagganak.

"I know Krat!"

They started shouting, and Lagganak's lightning sword, a famous blade of ancient Whitehall, was ignored before his question of Krat.

The dragon's head of goblin hate blinked in Bloodharvest, and its long tongue flicked through the stone halls of the prison. It heard lightning, but when it tasted, it found broken Krat. The flat-eyed serpent blinked. Rumors slithered through the rocks, biting the ears of dour goblins going about their business apathetically. They talked. Some came up to the ground floor and found Lagganak demanding an answer to a question no one had thought to ask.

"Of course, she's dead," they agreed. "The Black-tongues came for Bloodharvest, and she would have denied them."

"But do you know she died in Krat?" demanded Lagganak. "Why can no one assure me she died in Krat?"

As the jailers left their posts, I stole keys and went to the elves.

"Get ready. We make a run up and out," I said to Aehr. I unlocked those on the walls and their comrades hoisted each other up. The unchained made an injured crowd behind me, lifting each elf down from the wall as I unlocked them and lifting those chained to the floor to their feet. I unbound someone who whispered "thank you" with half a tongue, and I remembered her. There was no time. The next elf would have fallen from the wall if his withered comrades hadn't caught him. His legs were broken in many places, and he was scheduled to be a limper. We had to move. I unlocked the rest of Prince Aehr's people.

"What of Othrak?" the prince asked. His people gathered behind him.

I stared at him. "Prince, think before you speak. Othrak has been put to the Blackdrop. The only end is the Well of Memory. He's not coming out."

"I won't leave without him," said Aehr.

I chewed my lips.

"Prince, I've listened to Laptra and Thern. Othrak didn't help you. He did it for fame, to be known. He did it as a raised fist at Throathurters and goblins all. He wasn't some good figure, unjustly imprisoned. He's known. He got what he wanted."

Aehr looked at me curiously. "Why does that matter?"

"Because he wasn't doing anything to be nice! He only helped you to get something in return. It was a business deal, and one I've got no part in."

Aehr still looked confused. He indicated an elf who couldn't stand unaided. "But none of that mattered to us. This is Horase. He was beaten for not running when called. Othrak caught the fist that would have ended him. Now Horase lives. We labored without staving timbers. The mine collapsed, and all of us would have died. Othrak led us out. Did he brag? Yes. Are we dead? No. What do I care if he bragged?"

"Because you're all going to die if we go into the Well of Memory and taunt the Hungry Silence!" I yelled. "Othrak didn't help you out of kindness! He did it for spite!"

"Astrologamage Elegy, you speak of Othrak. We respect that. But I am Prince Aehr. I speak of elves. When the other doesn't deserve kindness, doing kindness is the greatest mark of character. I promised to remember him. If all you say is true, if he lays no bond on my word, if I keep or forget him purely as a mark of who I am, then I deserve to be someone who keeps his promises."

I glared at Aehr and the others. "And all of them? They deserve to die?"

The prince paused. That caught him the way I hadn't, and he hesitated. For a moment, he looked back.

"Astrologamage," said a gaunt elf in the back. Mute shuffling made an aisle for him, but he didn't walk forward. "You are of the race of Dread. Your kind has done terrible things to be famous. Is it so bad a goblin would do a kind thing for the same?"

Oh, damn, he threw that at me.

"But Dread was a bad guy," I argued faintly.

"For killing. Not for being famous."

We shared a long elvish silence, a drawn-out pause that would have been judgmental among humans. The elves waited. Aehr was torn by his own decision, but looked back to the gaunt elf. The gaunt one showed absolute certainty. Finally, the prince seemed to strengthen and turned back to me. His people filled in the aisle so they stood as one mass.

We were speaking Elvish, and I said a few humanisms that don't really translate. Aehr was going to get his way. Ah! I gain nothing by losing, so I might as well gain by agreeing.

"We are going down. We will go past the iron wall into the deep places of the Hungry Silence. They are attracted to noise and come rushing to blot it out. When we get to the Well, I will leave you and lower Othrak. He is riveted in an iron cage." My plan ended. There was no next step. "Let's go."

◆

The Blacktongues had left their lanterns by the wall and disappeared up the hall. I could hear them arguing. Thern lay where he had fallen, left for being weak enough to die. We took their lanterns and hurried to the Well of Memory. "Hurried," I say. Most of the elves could walk. Carrying the broad goblin lanterns, they had the pace of snails. They made as much noise, though. No speaking, no complaining; even their labored breathing was soft and hidden in the oily dark. Scratched runes on goblin lanterns smeared the light down here. When the elves moved closer to help themselves, they didn't step into the light, but surfaced and let shadows drain off them. When we arrived at the Well where Thern and Laptra had fought, the ground was still littered with bells. The water frothed and leaped, and the two cages hung perversely still. I pointed them out.

"He'll come down there." I stared at the elves, the cages, the rivets that still remained on the cages. There were no bones. "Good luck. I'll be back."

The lanterns wouldn't burn forever. Goblin lanterns burn dim, so the elves would survive the darkness for hours, maybe half a day, but the lights would die and shadows would rise. The Silence would creep in. It was coming.

They sat in a circle, resting, and held the lanterns firm against the night. Beyond them the shadows were still. Nothing moved. Nothing hungered.

Luthas

After leaving Aehr, instead of going up to Othrak, Bloodharvest, or the hills, I moved to a corridor and took a four-pane lantern of my own from my cloak. I'd stolen it a while ago; I can't remember who from. It was marked with sigils to survive the Silence, ugly scratchings that had turned the glass yellow like some corrosion was rusting the panes. The yellow stranger had drawn them in water on a table, and said they must be drawn on a lantern I hadn't paid for. The marks resembled water dropping onto the bottom of the pane and splashing against the lead. I lit the wick from an old flint and my right upper-forearm knife. It was the one I'd stabbed Thern with. Chips ruined the blade. The lantern wick barely caught flame and danced. My shadows danced with it. I curled up with my head in my hands and cried.

Othrak was going to die. Nothing could be done. If I made a miracle and lowered him, the chains could not be undone nor the rivets unbolted. Injured, near death, the elves had no strength for blacksmithing. They'd been sailors. They were all mostly dead.

If I made a miracle, how much noise would the miracle make? The miracle, how loud would it be? Where would the echoes go but down, into the deeps, where the Silence hid? It was down there now. Luthas's kind lived here. I felt they were sleeping lightly, merely dozing after the first alarm of the morning, before they went to work on Bloodharvest.

They were coming.

I had no boat. There were forty-three elves.

The lantern threw leaping shadows. I wept.

I wasn't so much done as interrupted when a sudden feeling of incredible dread shocked me out of my tears. Looking up, I saw Luthas staring at me.

"Hello, child," he whispered, genteel lips and teeth pressing through the smooth flesh over the front of his head. Skin pulled taut around them like wet gauze.

He was as tall as a goblin, with their long limbs and big head, but he had no face. The front of his head looked like a plump belly. Every time he spoke, a mouth and teeth pressed forward, stretching the hairless skin. Neither nose nor eyes appeared, but those lips and teeth spoke, wrapped in skin.

"How did you get through?" I asked. The small lantern flame leaped, but Luthas stood before a circle of light. The splashing sigil tumbled against the stone, and a trick of angle made it look like he was dripping into the dark outside the beam.

"Oh, child, I'm not like them," whispered Luthas. He waved at the further darkness. "I'm a friend! The sign doesn't repel friends." He put a gentle hand on the lantern.

I looked at the sharp smile pushing through the skin over his face, the lantern, and the deep catacombs under

Bloodharvest. I could run, but I'd leave the lantern. I'd be in the dark, with no sign, in the Silence.

"Friends are good," I said.

"We are." Teeth behind flesh smiled. "Friends."

We smiled at each other.

"I didn't catch your name before," he told me.

"Lehigh," I said.

"Lehigh." Teeth pushed forward as lips drew his skin tight. I felt an impression of marvelous hunger. "Thank you for giving me your name, and for that kind service you rendered me before. You moved my heart. I would like to give you a gift."

Oh, sweet humanisms, that was bad.

"Here. With my blessings," he said, and laid a small knife by the lantern.

I thought about old lore. Long ago, during times when Bloodharvest was built, the ancient kingdom of Whitehall had taken power from the warring tribes with a rigid code of conduct which, bent by Dread and Whitehall's fall, became Krat. Gift rules were now forgotten as unnecessary. In the old days, though, ingratitude was a terrible offense, one that justified incredible acts of vengeance. The ungracious could be hunted without mercy, and his name destroyed. (The goblin word for destroy and eat are the same.) I didn't know if any of those applied to Luthas. Yet he was here, giving gifts, and much as I didn't want to say anything, taking the knife under false pretenses was the sort of thing old goblins would chase you to the ends of Pallas for. Spurning a gift was the stuff of legends. Goblins made legends of suffering.

I smiled. "Thank you. You honor me."

"You are welcome. It pleases me you judge my gift worthy of the honor of your name."

Not good! I wanted to scream.

Instead I stared with jaw locked open, trying to out-think the dark, but Luthas only pressed his smile through the blank skin until veins bulged on his jaw. His teeth were too wide for the plane of his head, and his incisors marched past his cheekbones into hair. He bowed and sank out of the light.

I was left with his gift. The small knife's blade was but a hand's breadth long, as thin as my index finger. Neither edge differed from the other. The point was mundane. The metal was black as shadows until I held it to the light to inspect it. The gleam of the glass sign lit up imperfections in the steel like an unknown constellation.

With cold fingers, I put the blade to the floor and shaved a curl of stone, a tissue wave of granite that wound into a limitless spiral. In the dark, I couldn't see the curl's beginning or end. The cut left a sort of smear on the floor, but when I inspected it with the lantern, holding the light close with morbid curiosity, the smear resolved to merely stone. I inspected the knife. Granite ruins steel edges, and this granite was impregnated with smaller rocks and crystals. The blade should look like burlap. This thing was ready to cut God. I didn't test it with my thumb. Kindly, Luthas had left a sheath.

This was going to be bad.

Haeldrake

Bloodharvest's gates leading out of the deeps remained locked as the elves and I had left them. Thern still lay in a pile where he'd died. The Blacktongue looked at first like a dim pile of refuse. Up close his body formed itself out of shadow, with blood and fluids making his yellow robes look tattered. Little bits of chain speckled the walls. We'd taken the lanterns from where they'd been cast aside. Right now, knowing but not looking forward to what was to come, I stayed a moment at the gate. It was iron and steel on self-closing hinges with a hook catch. The latch was inside, but Thern had opened it easily by reaching through. Steel patterns of linked circles were carved into the floor. Blood that seeped out of Thern followed the grooves and turned them black. Indistinct echoes rolled down the hallways from upstairs. I unlocked the gate and went through, shutting it behind me against the dark.

Up the hall where the Blacktongues had argued, the ground was scraped. The shouting match had sounded chaotic, and footprints were a confused mass. I couldn't find groups that formed sides. Several scuff marks by a bit of tumbled stone confused me until, in sudden inspiration, I guessed they were left by a bored goblin sitting down and kicking his feet. Other footprints marked animated movement but not clearly enough to follow. The only place the footprints made sense was at a killing. Chains bound a dead Throathurter to the wall, and she had been ripped to pieces. The footprints all gathered as one around her.

I wanted to go up, get away from the deeps, but the way she had been killed confused me. For a while I stared. I reached out my arms and measured spans against the wall, trying to upsize for longer goblin arms. In Krat, all fights are one-on-one. They may follow each other closely, but thirty back-to-back fights are allowed. Tiredness is weakness, and Krat defies weakness. All fights are one-on-one, and this Throathurter had been ripped apart by a group. I stared, seeing something that had never cracked shatter.

From here, Blacktongues had killed their way upward. Throathurters, caught in various positions of surprise, were either ripped apart or mashed down. They looked like wet coffee grounds. Sometimes limbs remained. The section gates were closed and webbed in rusty steel chain. I put the knife of Luthas to use cutting my way in.

Further upstairs, I finally heard screaming, and I stood and listened. This wasn't my fight. I tried to outthink Othrak's cage, hanging a good leap from old, rickety catwalks. I guessed some rope trick might be possible, but as I sat in the dark, violence above and the goblin who had found fame below, I just couldn't believe I would get him out by jumping. The winch room was beyond all of Bloodharvest, and that would require stealth in the shallow dark.

I felt like I was stepping off a cliff when I extinguished my lantern. Its fractured yellow light was vaguely comforting, but shaded bonfires lit the highest of the underground levels. After the True Dark, they were floodlights. Stealth wasn't as welcoming as it usually was, but then again, that was how it was to be. I crept upward. Someone died shrieking.

At the border of the used prison holes, where goblin prisoners were worked to death, I came on wardens slaughtering their charges, strangling them in the darkness while the emaciated prisoners struggled. Thin feet kicked darkly on the stone, jerking against the rusty manacles. The prisoners gurgled and cried, and their own clan silenced them.

"Don't let the Blacktongues have them!" hissed a jailer.

I reached out of the dark, grabbed him, and sliced once. The back of his neck opened like a fish. The other guards didn't notice, until one looked up from his own killing and shrieked. The dead guard was all but gone— only his long arms and long fingers remained in the light, clutching with dead strength at the stone as I dragged him into darkness with me.

"I am Maru Ghostheart," I whispered. "We dead walk this place, feeding on those who feed us. Run."

Two of the guards ran. The last tried to finish his work, and in the shadows I took him. While the prisoners shrieked and covered their eyes, I cut the main links of their chains. I threw the keys among them and departed.

Fine. I would earn my pay.

Throughout the grim ascent, Throathurters killed their prisoners so the Blacktongues couldn't get them. They silenced their own shellings lest Blacktongues raise them wrong. That was too much. But with a foot down that path, I couldn't turn back, and the rest of the ascent was knife work.

At the main hall, one in a network of broad hallways that carried the voluntary residents, Blacktongues met dozens of Throathurters who were fleeing the pens in terror. They hit each other like madness. Blacktongues charged, screaming iron and steel in clattering ropes, and expected Throathurters to turn and run. But the Throathurters saw Blacktongues in every shadow and thought themselves trapped. They charged the enemy they could see, ripping iron links out of the air. The room exploded into noise—shrieking, breaking, and the peculiar sound of bleeding when pressurized skin breaks. In passing, I tipped over one of their oil braziers. It hit the ground and blew up into sheets of flame. Now they couldn't see. I kept going, heading for the winch chamber.

I made it, but the fighting followed into the old guardroom. It chased me on goblin legs with goblin hands, chains, and goblin yells. I couldn't even shut the door behind me, but bent to work as they fought. With goblins dying outside, I cut into the winch. The blade of Luthas cut too well, and I worked carefully, exposing chain and gears. With my heart thudding, I lit the lantern and shuttered it as much as possible, putting a single ray of amber light on the gears as I studied them. This interfaced with that; this thing drove that thing. I compared Othrak's winch with the others. Goblins just kept murdering each other outside. My teeth clenched a little tighter with each scream. Finally, I realized the spring-loaded triggers weren't brakes but catches, and the cages weren't meant to be lowered smoothly. They dropped and slammed in bone-breaking stages to the bottom. But I knew how to beat the goblins when I blew out the lantern.

By cutting pins and pinching springs, I lowered Othrak, letting him drop as fast as his emaciated body could endure. It wasn't fast enough; while there remained much chain to be lowered, a beaten, bleeding, burned Blacktongue dragged himself in. His eyes were full of blood, but he was thick and fed. I ghosted behind another winch and hid.

"You tried to snatch a shelling and run, ghost. Oh, human, you thought you were so fast," he whispered. Bile seeped out of his torso wounds, dripping down loops of chain that hung from his cuts like jewelry. He smelled vile. Goblin blood is bitter, and the winch room stank of it from the violence outside. "You thought, you thought, you thought you had the shelling.

"You never got away with anything, human. Hael-drake never didn't know. But we did the wise thing in the True Dark, and you thought we were stupid. But I have you, ghost. I have you in the shallow dark. I have you here. Because I heard Thern tell of the one, and Thern who argued for the drop died bleeding, and the cowards of Bloodharvest have whispered of a ghost in the dark. They whispered of a ghost in the border-lands of shadow, and here the door is open, and light outside fights the rising dark of the Blackdrop—" He babbled. His voice was unhinged, his jaws flapped too swiftly, and his tongue shut his nostrils when he talked too long, too fast. Mad Haeldrake sputtered and bled as gall bubbled out of his cuts. He sounded like he was talking to himself. I stayed quiet and hidden. The stink outside was overwhelming.

"But Blacktongues aren't stupid, human." He gasped. Poor cadence left him breathless. He had to slow down to breathe. "We weren't unaware you were after a shelling. We let you, because we had to be smart in the True Dark. And it is you who are stupid. Because you were so certain you were the smart human, you came here. And I knew. I know."

Haeldrake gasped again. Still, he talked too fast to breathe. He reached out above me. From below their arms are freakishly long. He looked like a marionette on strings.

"I see your lantern," whispered Haeldrake. Anger locked up his jaw, but it let him breathe. His puppet hand picked up my lantern in long grasping fingers, and he whispered, "And it's still hot."

He dropped my stolen lantern down the winch pit. It never bounced, and if tumbled off the walls, it did so beyond hearing.

The gloom outside still hung his silhouette in the doorway, and a black outline of a thin arm reached across the doorway like a bar. I thought he was going to block the way with his arms. He didn't. He took the door and shut it like a parent putting a child to bed. But he was in here with me, and I had no surprise.

He breathed once, twice, and stilled, nothing compared to the havoc in the hallway outside and the faint breath of air up from the deeps below.

I hid and listened.

Underneath ringing violence, even dampened by the door, a long bare foot pressed leather skin to the floor. It twisted and stopped. I heard him sniffing.

Oh, no.

A sudden burst of fighting drowned the room noise out, and I lost him. I gauged the wind. The hole in the floor sourced a steady but weak current that wrapped up between the winches and out a vent over the door. Between machinery the air slashed into crosscurrents. Haeldrake could be anywhere.

I began to feel the urge to move, to not sit still, which is the deadly enemy of stealth. I can be quieter than the dark when I'm still, but any movement could cast a noise, to say nothing of the abyssal pit that led to fatal reunion with Aehr. My gut said otherwise. Haeldrake sniffed again. I couldn't place it. He was so quiet the sound of sniffing danced with the wind. That sniff could be anywhere, unlike the first one. I at least had known where the first sniff was—which meant he had moved.

If I moved, I could hit him. Imagine placing a bare hand down and finding bloody goblin skin. Imagine Haeldrake coming toward me. He could be terribly close right now, above me, looking down, sniffing. Imagine he was inside my space in front of my face, listening, breathing through long, wet teeth.

In my mind, I walked over to terrified Elegy, patted her on the head, and politely told her to sit down and eat a cookie. Terrified Elegy screamed and ran in circles, shaking her little arms. I let her bang into a wall, fall down, and then put the cookie on her lap so she could hush up.

Goblins can't smell that well. Goblins tend to be dirty by human standards exactly because they can't smell themselves, and they don't demand perfume like we do for the same reason. Haeldrake was sniffing for me, but the worst thing to do was panic and give away my position. He couldn't smell well, but that doesn't mean he couldn't smell at all. In time, in the small area, he might be able to find me. I did have to move, but I had to be smart.

I sniffed, gently, lightly, like I was alone before a date and wanted to be sure nothing in the air was me. I caught hints of goblin and rust, but nothing localized.

I sniffed again. The wind from below carried no odor, and the winches and drives broke each gust into fragments. They carried metal in fractured pathways. To get useful information, I needed to sniff air that was full of useful information, and where it was moving predictably. The vent over the door carried all the air out of the room. In silence that made the shadows loud, I went around the deadly fall and felt the air on the bare skin of my hands. I noted the light under the door. I crept along a wall toward the doorway, and listened so hard my own pulse thundered in my ears.

At the door, I waited until I felt certain and sniffed.

"Hello," whispered Haeldrake, his hot breath on my lips and his fangs wetting my inhales.

I snatched my knife, and he snatched me, long arms grasping as he caught me by the wrists. I kicked, he dodged, and then he opened his mouth to scream in steel, a smashing echo of metal that wrapped and bound me while outside my silhouette chains thundered against the wall. Steel banged on stone. I snatched the knife of Luthas from my wrist, but Haeldrake screamed again, yanking my arms wide. He threw me through the door. I hit and slid on ground drenched in the clan battle.

It was a madness of fire and death out here, a wasteland where dead goblins were packed into drifts. They had torn each other apart, rending limbs from torsos. Chain hung from the ceiling like spiderwebs. It stuck where it hit with a glue of rust and spit. I struggled as Haeldrake stalked out behind me. Nearly three meters tall, he wiped vomitous steel from his mouth like a bit of dinner from a messy roast. His arms and legs were longer than I was tall. The room stank of burned flesh.

"Ghost," he said. "Ghosts can't be tied!"

"Ah, but for cold iron!" I lied, and started cutting the chain on my wrist.

"Then brass!" he screamed, and green metal tore from his mouth. Links hit like fists, knocking me back and down. His tongue wiped his lips and lay down, hanging over the edge of his mouth. "You cannot remove the brass either! You are wrong, and I won!" He laughed and broke into coughing.

When he could, he gasped between pants, "Bloodharvest for the Blacktongues!" "The death of Throathurters and you!" His chest heaved and buckled as he strained to breathe.

"Bloodharvest for me!"

Both of us looked, Haeldrake whirling and me craning my neck, and Lagganak stood in the doorway. His body was a mass of blood and burns, and the Departing crackled at his side. The blade skittered in its sheath.

"What thing are you?" demanded Haeldrake. I reached for the knife of Luthas. It was gone. A wristband I wear to stuff reeds into had a buckle by my thumb, and I worked that loose with a finger. I started picking at the multiplied chains that bound me. They weren't tied; there were just a lot of them, metal that connected me to Haeldrake. Lagganak bore Melbrod, a sword of lightning.

Live by the bet, die by the bet. I had bet my life a few times that Lagganak would use the lightning sword whenever he could, even when it wasn't to his advantage. It had worked. Now I was bound by metal to Haeldrake. I worked furiously at the chains, hoping the voices of panic in my head would see I was too busy for them.

"Lagganak of Thunderblood," Bent Hands replied. For a split second, he and Haeldrake sized each other up. Lagganak spoke first.

"I'd like to thank you. You answered a question for me. All my life I wondered about hiding who I am, working among the Throathurters. I swallowed bile and suckled poison. I kept it down. And I always wondered what it would be like to exist freely, to throw off my chains, to excrete the same violence I endured. What would happen if I ignored Krat, and just killed?

"You answered that. You violate law. You twist Krat. Act without restraint, kill without thought, you do. All my life, I've fought the insufferable desire to do without thinking, and you don't. You fight. I can see, perfectly, what I would become if I did what I've always wanted. You are my answer.

"And the truth is, you're weak." Lagganak spoke slowly, pouring a lifetime of swallowed bitterness into the contempt of that one word. "You're small. You make Krat less by your actions. You harm the Throathurters. Generations from now, the shame of your actions will cripple your clan, forbearing them from standing at Grosjean. Goblins who strive toward a life of honor have been hamstrung by your actions in their name. Till the end of days, Blacktongue and treason will be one word, until your clan is shamed into submitting to a new master. Your shame is weakness. But you have claimed to be strong in Krat while your honor is flaccid, and Krat requires a price for that. I will sell you your honor for the manner of your death."

"Never," swore Haeldrake, eyes wide. He hissed, and tiny snakeheads of steel lifted from the edges of his mouth like baby vipers.

"Come! Is not all possible in honor? Even you can regain your name!"

"I am forever!"

"Forever weak!"

I finally got my right hand free, rolled over, snatched Luthas's blade from the ground and cut my bonds. I peeled bloody steel from my hands and wrists. Panic whispered to me. I got free. The walls dripped iron chain; the floor had pools of rust and blood. The Thunderblood carried Melbrod, the sword of lightning.

Haeldrake began to inhale. Wind tugged my hair, the loose ends of my robes that dangled to break my outlines. Deeper scents of blood and gore rushed from the killed to the Blacktongue. Lagganak hissed. He spread his feet. Even sheathed, Melbrod crackled with power. I scented ozone under the goblin excreta, and the two scents fought for dominance.

"Blacktongue!" screamed Haeldrake. His word was a metal storm.

"Krat!" shrieked Lagganak, and drew the sword.

They hit each with a detonation as I ran into the winch room, sliced the grate in half, and dove down the Blackdrop with falling metal. Chain, lightning, and blood exploded.

The Dream in Emerald

The elves hauled me out of the bubbling pit. I don't know if I lost consciousness when I hit, or if I fainted during the fall. Even now, I can't remember the feeling of that fall. It was too long. I'm aware that I plummeted for multiple breaths. I fell, inhaled, held it, kept falling, exhaled, kept falling, and needed air. I remember that burn of empty lungs during the fall. I had to breathe again and again while I fell, but I can't remember the feeling of falling so long that breathing mattered. I don't remember hitting the water.

"You are lucky," said Aehr as they dragged me out. Oddly enough, I remember that. When elvish hands held me, their fingers caught on my bracelets. Water got under the leather, where my skin was still dry. A splash put bubbles on Aehr's face, and a big one ran down his nose to hang between his nostrils. "This is the Artificer's Well, drawn from the rootwaters of the Arsae. We are under the tree ocean. The water here does something we do not fully understand. Your fall does not seem to have harmed you, and the water accepted you without taking a flesh toll."

I looked around. Othrak's cage rested on the stones outside the pool, and walking elves tended him. He was flailing weakly.

"I also didn't hit that," I said.

Aehr looked amused. "Of course. We moved quickly lest he drown."

I got up and checked myself over. Nothing new hurt. I noticed some bruises and cuts from when Haeldrake grabbed me. My ankles ached from a minor injury I had sustained stopping Throathurters from strangling children. I shook it out.

Othrak's cage was old metal. Luthas's blade cut it apart, and we pulled the withered goblin out. Elves scooped water with their hands, carried it to him, and poured it down his lips. Prince Aehr held his head as Othrak gasped. Some of the elves looked at each other, and more than a few regarded Aehr with varying levels of doubt. Prince Aehr could not have cared less. They gave the goblin water until he wanted no more, and an honor guard helped him to his feet. Tall elves stood as high as his waist, and he leaned until they were carrying him with his feet moving.

I was pleased to see the lanterns were still lit and strong. The limpers and carried elves tended them.

Outside, the Hungry Silence moved. It did not break the line of light, but waves of it pushed quietly into view, broke against Blacktongue runes, and left a foam of shadow within the circles of light. It waited.

"Good. We're all here, and in the darkness, we're going to die," I said.

Aehr shook his head. "No, we won't. Come. We have found means of escape."

"What?" I demanded, shaking spray from my head.

Aehr looked at me curiously and switched to formal Celephian. The court language in the Crystal City sounded like bastardized slang. "Are you quite well?"

"Fine. Fine. Escape?"

"You know that Laptra Throathurter had encouraged Brand the Artificer to make his domicile here? Encouraged, flattered, and then imprisoned? You also know he is not here now?"

"Yes, yes." That all seemed familiar.

"We have found his labor."

"And we can escape?"

"Yes. I will show you."

"Oh. Nice."

"Walk carefully. You may have hit your head." He diffidently touched my arm for stability.

"No, no. I've been concussed before. This is just adrenaline wearing off. Things got a little shady up there." I waved him off.

The Prince didn't look convinced, but he didn't argue. Elves, you know. I followed him, and the elves followed, some carrying the injured, some lifting lanterns high.

Aehr told me the elves had waited for a while by the pool. Nothing had awoken. With unusual impatience, they had taken to looking around. The bottom of the Well of Memory was a broad, cylindrical chamber with a lower ceiling, 140, 150 feet high, around the central well. Hallways opened to outside spaces. Some of them were storerooms, some empty, some filled. Some doorways were corridors than led elsewhere into darkness.

The elves had not explored far. Close by, they had found the Artificer's laboratory.

It was here they led me. Many lanterns already burned when we arrived. A rest area with old food was prepared. We ate goblin food. Most was stale, unleavened bread that would keep halfway to forever, and much of this was wrapped in wax. When the stars died, this stuff would be no less edible than it was right now. Everyone had eaten some, and they made a paste for Othrak. Goblin food isn't good or bad. It's sustenance for people who find the idea of eating annoying.

The great thing about the Artificer's laboratory was that it wasn't dark. For the first time since I arrived, I could see easily. There were lanterns on the walls, torches in brass fittings, and several broad chandeliers with wicks that hung from platters of oil. Those were interesting. The flames burned at the lowest part of the wick. They looked like fruit. But they cast light everywhere, and the ceilings, walls, and doors were all plainly visible.

As this had been nominally a prison, the doors were also barred with iron. That made me feel better.

Inside the first room of the lab were a number of gears and gear chains, a complex orrery that represented the sky as it spun over the disk of Pallas, but what dominated was water. There were thousands of tubes, bottles, and glass flow-ways of water on desks, leaping from desk to desk and running through the walls and sometimes underfoot. Glass vessels near the entrance opened their mouths, and a line of buckets hung neatly from the walls.

A little checklist kept track of water added to the accepticle by unit time, jotted in neat handwriting three feet above my head. Goblins must have done it. Somewhy that amused me. Bottles open to the air had run dry, but many still held water or aqueous solutions, a few bubbling. I tapped one that boiled merrily in a crystal globe: skin temperature.

"Is this rootwater? Have you tried adding more?" I asked Aehr.

"No. We declined to disturb the Artificer's work."

"Probably wise." I guess. I was curious what would happen.

"Let us rest a moment, and I will show you the escape," said Aehr. His people were taking a breather, and Othrak lay sprawled out. He looked dead. Horase ate slowly, soaking bread in water until it dissolved in his mouth. He didn't have the strength to chew. The elf with half a tongue leaned against a wall. I asked her name, and she told me she would be Alsace from Alsette. She couldn't pronounce the latter anymore. I nodded and chewed on tack. It tasted like chalk.

Chalk isn't that bad. I know people who complain about food by comparing it to chalk, but chalk isn't actively distasteful, it's merely not good. That was goblin food. I wondered if it had anything to do with their nostril positioning. I'd ask Othrak.

The first room of the Artificer's lab had been so devoted to fluid chemistry that I was surprised the second was devoted to weather. Thunderstorms raged in bottles with cork stoppers charred by spiderwebs of lightning. Another had a small rock and a smaller rock orbiting it, bound together by two hairs of rain. Up close the raindrops fell from one rock toward another, never quite touching, to be slung around and back. Some splattered against the bottle glass and dripped to the bottom, where they collected into rings. A third bottle, twice my height, was half full of thyf and so wet it rippled when I tapped the bottle. The thyf jiggled disturbingly, mounding up, hesitating, and receding, as the minuscule fronds of the tiny ferns rushed under my fingers. I didn't put my face against it to look. Two small waterspouts cut circles in the thyf and rose up and smashed into each other. For a while the bottle was quiet.

"Come, come," urged Aehr. I followed him out the back door.

The next room had a lizard skull the size of a wagon, wired up with gears to rise and hiss as we walked through. In the next, a fireplace sizzled merrily in a mirror behind a cold hearth. When I leaned in close, I saw my reflection blink. A fountain poured thick yellow liquid from a cherub's cornucopia. It smelled suspiciously like maple syrup.

Prince Aehr urged me again. It was like the elven race had suddenly discovered time as soon as there was something worth looking at.

He badgered me through the next door and waved at his prize, grinning impishly. He looked tiny, proud, and strong. I looked at him before what he was pointing at, noticing the way his features stood out under candlelight.

This was the first time I'd actually seen him illuminated. Always before we'd been in jail or the deeps, where the shadows formed an oily stain that our slim lanterns hadn't been able to repel. Aehr was a good-looking little man. He had a strong jawline and sharp features. The pointed ears were a little weird, but they suited him. His eyes were deep brown, flecked with green, and though he never stood exactly straight, his ever-so-slight bend to the side was as natural as the rest of him. He obviously wasn't human, but the ways in which he wasn't human agreed with each other. He looked consistent and stable.

I looked where he was pointing and nearly soiled my pantaloons. The Artificer had made a ship.

He'd made a ship, but he used the plans for a dragon. Possessing a startling unconcern for the laws of custom and nature, the Artificer's *Dream in Emerald* carried her sails on the sides. Her hull was a dozen skis that overlapped like scales. She had a snarling head for a prow; her eyebrow ridges carried two rows with forward pennants, emerald on emerald on staves of green. Her teeth were long, and a furnace lit her emerald eyes, ready to bathe her jaws in oil fire. The back of the ship was a jointed tail more than half the vessel's total length that slithered side to side in cradle. The whole thing was magnificent, monstrous. As a faint wind hissed through iron grates from outside, leaking in from the submerged depths of the Arsae to skitter around the *Dream in Emerald*, she squirmed inside her moorings. Her name was written on her prow.

I put a hand up, for she lay dry-docked some slight distance above the head, and traced lacquer-work scales that marched like shields from nose to tail. She was smooth as a snake's underbelly.

"We can sail right out of here," I whispered.

"Our escape is at hand," agreed Aehr, bubbling with excitement.

I grinned at him. He smiled back.

"Beautiful ship," I said.

He beamed. "Captain Elegy, shall you board?"

"Not Captain, just Astrologamage," I replied, beaming myself.

"But you'll sail her."

"No, I won't. You'll sail her."

Aehr's smile cracked. "I can't sail her."

"What do you mean you can't? What about your ship? Is it broken or gone?"

"I am not sure what ship you mean," said Aehr.

"The one they caught you on. You and your sailors." I indicated the other elves absently.

"We were not on a ship."

I looked at him. Aehr's eyes were very wide.

"You weren't sailing?"

"No, Astrologamage Elegy. We were not."

A long silence ensued. The elvish comfort with long silences threw off my instincts. I wanted to wait so he would feel inclined to speak and tell me something, but he was an elf. They weren't bothered by pauses. He would outwait me without knowing he was doing it. He had no patience before, but now he had all the time in the world.

"How were you captured?" I asked.

"We were walking. We circumnavigated the Karas to the west and entered goblin territory."

Why in God's Holy Name would any jackass waltz into goblin territory—why would an elvish prince waltz into goblin—what in—was he stupid?

"Why did you do that?" I asked.

"We're biologists. We were following wolves."

I stared at him so hostilely he explained. Either that or he just wanted to talk biology.

"The wolves have left the Solange. Few even remain in the Languid. The creatures of the forest breed to excess, which kills the trees, and they starve and suffer. There are no wolves to restrain them. The wolves have gone north."

Aehr lapsed into a discussion of breeding rates, population pressures, and long term functional instability. None of it passed my ears.

This elf had wandered into goblindom, had been captured by goblins and sent to Bloodharvest. He was here because he had followed wolves. Don't the goblins still mark their borders with impaled creatures? They've done it ever since Dread, to tell the world they're willing to do unto others as has been done unto them. Did he miss it?

"Excuse me, excuse me." I interrupted him. He looked displeased. "Did you miss the warnings? Dead people on spikes?"

"We went around them."

I've never actually had my jaw fall open before. I've heard about it, but I had never gone slack-jawed. Several impolite seconds later, I noticed my mouth was open when Aehr looked down to my mouth and back. I shut my mouth and my teeth clicked.

They had not accidentally entered goblin territory. They had walked around the impalements.

I rubbed my eyes. I massaged my temples. I stared philosophically into the ether. I didn't smack anyone.

"Well," I said, to get my mind moving. "That's going to raise certain problems for us. I don't sail. You don't sail. Do any of the other prisoners sail?"

"No," he said.

Of course not.

"Is that a problem?" he asked.

I stared upward. Who would be around here? Goblins. There would be goblins. Goblins sailed thunderheads over the Arsae. They would probably be disinclined to help. We had a goblin: Othrak. I wouldn't take odds he'd survive the night, much less bet my life he'd sail us south.

Whalers? Not over the Arsae Crests among the goblin-mounts. Elves don't come here much.

Terrors of the deep? There were definitely terrors of the deep. No. Just, no.

"Aehr, I'm not sure you recognize that no one is crazy enough to—Sweet Mercy."

"Is Sweet Mercy a person?" asked Aehr.

I looked at him. Aehr waited. Elvish patience.

"Is there anything around here that might be used to send a message?" I asked.

"There was a Mirror of Grim Reflections in the room past the dragon head," replied Aehr. "Who do you—"

"Mirror," I said.

Like everything else, the Mirror was made with water, but I didn't catch it at first because it was vertical. A pane of glass sandwiched a plane of water against a bronze backing. The water wasn't exactly still or perfectly transparent. If watched, one would notice distortions in the reflection, like when it appeared I was winking at myself, but these were slight and easy to ignore. Prince Aehr recognized the thing and said he knew of its type. They are not unknown in the Solange. The Mirror required fire in the cold hearth, and once set with the Artificer's oil, the water within danced. Bubbles kicked reflecting waves across the surface. They caught light between the glass and verdigrised brass, and trapped rainbows danced in the water. The rainbows of the glass were filled with green, and in combination, the glass seemed alive and growing.

"Can you call someone named Phillius?" I asked.

"Of course. A man?" He approached the glass.

"Elf."

Aehr glanced at me.

"It's an odd name," I replied dismissively.

Aehr frowned. His lips pursed. "It is a mannish name."

I shrugged. "Would you call him, please?"

The prince continued to frown, but turned and addressed the mirror. "I will need more than just a name. Give me some of his features or history."

I relaxed and thought back. "He's taller than you, very thin, very wiry. His fingers are long and sharp. His eyes lie like daggers behind the sheaths of his brow. He sailed with Jasper under Helen."

Aehr had been standing with his hands upraised, but he turned and lowered them. "He sailed with Jasper? Under Helen?"

I nodded. "Is that enough?"

"That is entirely too much," replied Aehr, and spoke a summoning into the water.

The prince sang softly, barely a whisper, within sharply banded ranges of tone. With rhythm, he formed melody on a fraction of a scale, rushing but little up or down. Yet with complex beat his voice sounded like many waterfalls tumbling down the steps. He established a pattern and from it dropped many lesser melodies. Other elves who had been speaking went silent. I could not understand the words. His hands danced quietly. The rainbows flared.

"Phillius," said Aehr, with an edge of fear. "He is on a boat."

"*Regret*," I said, and stepped forward to look into the reflection.

Aehr's speaking had deepened the rainbows, and the green patina on the bronze backing looked like sunset on leaves. He tapped the glass in time to his chant. Ripples made the leaves dance, and bubbles clouded the reflections. I kept looking as Aehr's reflection lost coherence. It shook until the foggy glass made it look quite a bit like a twisted elf on a fast boat, reveling in sailing the Arsae.

Phillius knew he was being watched. He looked up once, dead into my eyes, and returned to tending his sails. The broad rear edge of *Regret* kicked dovetails of thyf as it raced over the trees, and leaves bounced back from its weight to kick motes of dust into the air. Strong winds blew forward into the complex catches of the sails. Phillius raced a wind that outran him while the greatest canopy rushed behind. The rush of thyf in the wind over his face was indistinguishable from the green of tarnished brass in the Mirror of Grim Reflections.

I looked at Aehr. He scowled but pointed from his lips to the mirror while maintaining his chant. I took that to mean I could talk.

"Phillius, Astrologamage Elegy calls. I know you see me."

"I see and hear you. Have you died, ghost?"

Optimistically, I replied. "No. I need your help. I am with your prince and his people. We prepare to sail from Bloodharvest."

"Ah!" He smiled. "To sail from the goblinmounts! You amuse me. Do you have a ship?"

"I do. I need a captain."

"Ha! You did not look like much of a sailor. You turned green at a little play."

Phillius smiled and leaned hard against the wind. *Regret* lifted on one runner, catching wind as she hopped over the treetops.

"We have a ship," I repeated. "The *Dream in Emerald*. We need a master sailor to captain it."

"Her," corrected Phillius. He laughed as when the whales had played. "I will sail for you."

"Come to Bloodharvest, Captain. When you are here, we will launch. We may meet you on the treetops, perhaps under pursuit."

"Four days, woman. *Regret* is fast." Phillius winked and tended to his ropes. Aehr crossed a hand over the glass, and the contact faded.

Aehr glared up at me. "This is not a good plan, Astrologamage Elegy. Hiding in the Hungry Silence is one thing. Desperate times require desperate gambles. But I would rather roll dice then throw them into a fire, hoping they melt into pips."

"You wandered past impalements looking for wolves!"

"I know where to find a dead goblin if I want one. Those had nothing to do with me."

I had to turn and walk away.

The Calm

For a couple of days we rested. Aehr told me of his life. He'd spent most of his time in the sculpted wild of the Languid Forest, at first absorbed by a love of ants. He figured out how they track pathways, identified the difference between drones, workers, warriors, and queens, and dug up abandoned nests to study their chambers. He learned little tricks, too. With a paintbrush and sugar water, he could write his name in ants. The trick, he told me, as if this was great lore, was to write so the path out was sculpted as well. Too often he had started with glorious lettering and ended with a jumble. From names, he learned to write music with them, too.

"Sometimes I sing the melodies they write as they leave. They make dropping music, full of scales that plunge. Ants don't follow paths exactly, and a few wander off. I played the music as if each ant was actually a note wherever it was." He looked at me as I sprawled in a chair near him. My legs hung off the arms of the Artificer's chair, and fringes hung from my legs. I hadn't seen moss in so long I was using cut felt to break my outlines.

"When did you study wolves?" I asked.

"Never," he admitted. "I find the verna too interesting. The smaller creatures creep and run. Squirrels in a forest fly as well as sparrows in the air. Wolves will eat verna if they can, though they prefer moose and deer. But there are no wolves in the Languid now. I must know why."

I nodded. He stared at nothing, and I looked down at myself. The problem with dressing like a pile of dead leaves is you look like a pile of dead leaves. It's useful, but it can be frustrating.

The Mirror of Grim Reflections bubbled. For once it seethed. I expected it to calm down, but it foamed at the base. Low parts boiled. The usually green water was oddly black.

Aehr got up to look at it, and I moved close enough to snatch him if something tried to happen. We were so close to being done. The mirror frothed angrily. The clockwork skull hissed. I reached out, took Aehr by the arm, and pulled him away from the mirror.

"Get a little space," I said.

"It is—"

The glass shattered. Splinters tore the brass until it curled like chains and stank of rust. For a moment, a thousand tentacles of bleeding iron reached out of the mirror. They splashed on the stonework floor and became just a spill of rusty water.

"The last Blacktongue in Bloodharvest is dead," I said. "I'm sure of it."

"Does that affect us?" Aehr asked.

"In dying, some word was spoken that should have left the world unsaid. I think—" I hesitated. "I think the doorways from the lab to the Well of Memory, and indeed all doorways from the lab to the under-reaches of Bloodharvest, should be shut and sealed. We should move inward and keep lit rooms between us and the dark."

"Astrologamage Elegy?" His voice hinted at something.

I touched Luthas's blade. I kept it hidden up a sleeve, on the inside of a hidden bracelet.

"Do you know anything of sharks?" I asked.

"No," he admitted.

"They frenzy. Let's—let's stay on the boat. In the light. Let's stay on the boat in the light."

The ground shook, and the iron cages groaned where they were bolted to the walls. I started pushing people onto the boat.

We had plenty of the Karas rootwater and the meaningless goblin bread in good supply. We ate much and drank deeply without wasting anything. Elves put flesh on their bones. On the second day, they had begun walking without shaking. Othrak could talk without exhausting himself. We told him where we were and where we intended to go.

"The one does not revel in a journey to Elvenhome," he said when he could walk.

"Othrak, you will be well cared for," promised Aehr. "I remember."

Othrak nodded. "You remember well."

The next day, the third day after contacting Phillius, the outermost door of the Artificer's lab rattled inside the iron cage. It clicked and clanked. I went to the door between the weather room and the outer lab and looked out. When we had left, we'd filled the Artificer's lanterns, but they were burning down. The air smelled of old smoke and something pungent.

I locked the doors of the inner rooms and filled the artificer's lanterns, lit every candle, and set the chandeliers burning. No one else left the ship. In the quiet, the outer doors rattled faintly, little more than a finger testing a squeaky hinge.

I had the sudden, strangest urge to yell "hello." I did not.

We sealed every room save the dock room and figured out how to launch. The Artificer had put a mechanism together of winches and springs. Leaving would be simple. It would be as simple as falling off a cliff.

The clockwork dragon began to clank. It was morning on the fourth day.

We'd taken shards of the water mirror to the boat, and I robustly encouraged Aehr to try to contact Phillius. He partially succeeded. We could see the wiry elf sailing, ropes bound around his wrists as he leaned far overboard with body hanging from his ship. His face was drenched, and rain hit him like fists. Phillius's face was dark until thunder cracked it. He didn't respond when we called, and Aehr broke the connection.

"We have time," Aehr assured me.

Lights under the doors flickered unevenly. They stuttered like many people were moving in the far room. The mirror fragments were too tarnished to reflect dry, but Aehr dipped his in rootwater to try to contact his people. It showed his reflections, smiling with many teeth. Aehr said sometimes his reflection smiled when he did not. Aehr smiled a lot. It was probably coincidence.

"Those Blacktongue lanterns," I reminded him. "The ones with the sigils on them."

"They cannot be refilled. The vessel is glass and sealed to the wick holder."

I blinked at him.

"It prevents their lanterns from being used against them," Aehr said helpfully.

The thing is, he was right. That was goblin custom. Their sensitivity to light made lanterns weapons, to say nothing of the element of pride. 'We are Blacktongue, and we bring our own lanterns you cannot use.' I knew this. I had just forgotten goblindom.

"Well, light what you can," I said, and turned toward the door to the room with the clockwork dragon skull. I hadn't smelled maple syrup in some time.

Aehr tried to summon Phillius again on the mirror. He had better luck this time, a fraction of contact for the sailor to say, "I see the fist, but it is wrapped in lightning. This is too early for afternoon thunderstorms. This storm comes too early. Can you wait?"

The doorknob to the fireplace room turned; a soft voice asked "Lehigh?" at the doorway.

"No!" I said, and cut the final restraints.

◆

The shock of departure was almost relaxing. The *Dream in Emerald* caught clockwork and raced upward. Miles of segmented fingers dragged us along. Springs clacked as gears clanked, and our speed increased until the Artificer's work threw us out of the submerged side of the goblinmount into the deep foliage of the Arsae, among the roots of infinite trees.

They did not root in the ground but in masses of dirt and rock thousands of feet up, forming second canopies atop pillars of trunks. Power-rich rootwater tumbled from cracks in the mountain and the trees hunted those streams, filling the cracks with root and stem. Streams of falling mist tumbled from leaf and branch.

We hit the upper canopies like a meteor and crashed through the treetops and thyf into rain. The dragon flew. Lightning danced under the clouds and flowed like water to the Polyp. The rain didn't fall steady, but hammered, paused, and struck us again. Each wave stung. The *Dream in Emerald* soared for an instant above, and lightning curled around her, tasting her like a serpent's tongue. She slammed down, cut the forest, and nearly rolled over in the wind.

I explored my human vocabulary. We had rolled sideways vertical, and the deck was a rain-slicked cliff. "Elves to the high side!" I screamed. "Aehr to the steerage. Do something!"

Elves obeyed. They'd needed rest stops to go three rooms a few days ago, and now scrambled up soaked decking, hauling each other toward gunwales. Wind caught us in the keel and lifted, and the gunwales became rafters under the rain ceiling. The down side caught, and we skittered, bouncing. The high side sails were catching air, and they would have to be cut. Otherwise they'd drive us over.

We'd be dead on the forest if I cut the sails. We'd be dead in, through, and under the forest if I didn't. I preferred to die later. Much of the deck wasn't deck, but a wide lattice, to reduce weight. It acted like a ladder. I scrambled up and marked my cuts, when I saw movement in the thunder flashes.

The *Dream in Emerald* bounced across the treetops, splashing drenched thyf and breaking twigs, but the wind caught it so it couldn't quite slam. *Regret* came at us from the fore. As the *Dream in Emerald* tossed and rolled, Phillius sailed a straight line into her and stepped aboard through a shower of splinters as the Artificer's handiwork annihilated *Regret*.

"Well done, children," called Phillius. The madman scurried up the pilot's ladder and laid hands on the wheel.

We twisted, heaved, and laid down flat, running fast before the wind on our dragon-scale belly.

I goggled at Phillius for several seconds and then looked at Aehr. Luthas's knife was out and ready to cut rigging, but I hid it before anyone noticed.

The prince muttered, "This is still a bad idea," but no one who wasn't watching his lips could have understood him.

Phillius was taller than I remembered, as tall as I was. He was also leaner, somehow incorrect. Someone that lean should have bulged at the joints; they should be swollen at the elbows and wrists. Phillius wasn't. Phillius looked like 200 springs were bent against each other, and each one strove with body-breaking force to contract and break the rest. The spikes of his fingers wrapped the steerage, and the wood buckled under his skin.

We ran flat south before the wind, stealing gusts as they pleased us and slipping away from the rest. Treetops crashed before us, whipping their wet branches against the hull as we shot through, and it felt like real waves. We lurched and rushed like a corsair on the high seas. Phillius began to hum as the rain cut to my core.

And then we broke the outer limit of the thunderstorm and hit sunlight. The wind shifted hard. We tacked into it, and in a moment, we were soaking wet in sunshine, racing across the green froth of the Arsae, heading south toward the Arsae Crests.

"Naturally," I told Aehr, and shrugged that he had ever doubted me.

"You could not have planned that," he replied.

"Check my references. This is what I do." I winked at him.

Prince Aehr turned away, and we checked the elves.

They were all fine. Somehow, they'd kept their grips while the ship had tried to crash and endured. Mere horror hadn't stopped them. A few retained their holds on the deck, for sailing across the Arsae is a leaping, jolting process with much falling, but none of them were dead.

Aehr also checked on Othrak. The goblin was weak but alive, with his long arms wrapped around a central winch-point. He looked worse than anyone.

"Hey, you're looking much better!" I said.

His Highness ignored me. Aehr said to Othrak, "Do you see now, I have remembered?"

"The storm," Othrak whimpered.

"We have escaped it."

Othrak turned and looked at Aehr. His flat face was grayish green, and the short tusks that kept his lips parted when he slept were wet with rain.

"No, Prince Aehr, we have merely left it. That is a goblin storm."

For a moment, we all looked at him, and then forty-six pairs of eyes turned back.

On top of the great thunderhead, where the crown of the anvil reached up to smite the sky, the storm head unfurled the banner of the Throathurters: a goblin head twisting in goblin hands on a background of thunder and fire. Lightning leaped from the storm and flailed the sky. The booms rattled off the heavens. Goblins on the Polyp unmoored hawsers of lightning, which boomed as well, crackling and echoing between the forest and clouds. Swiftly the thunderhead parted from Bloodharvest and turned after us.

"Bad luck." Phillius grinned.

Bad Luck

The storm made its own wind, a raging mix of cross-currents that caught the sea beneath. Increased in power, the gale under the thunderhead ripped apart the canopy and shook the Arsae to its roots. Trees shook and beat each other as branches like great highways splintered and fell. They left abysses in the surface of the sea. Underneath the cloud was a death zone, and we fled before it.

Phillius began to hum some bouncing sea chantey. During breaks, he barked out crisp orders, though the *Dream in Emerald* mostly ran itself. The sails ran by gears, the hulls rose and lowered on tracks, and the mad elf took to all of them with perverse aptitude. The elves dashed from side to side on the ship, counterbalancing the weight of each turn, while I sat on a spar over the tail. Trees lashed back and forth under my feet. The heavy *Dream in Emerald* sailed lower than *Regret* had. She put my heels in thyf if I wasn't looking.

It was like being chased by a mountain. The thunderhead shouldered other, lesser clouds aside instead of absorbing them, and the lowly white puffballs tumbled out of its way. It threw a wake of sky foam a dozen miles wide until the winds caught the far ends, pushing them together and off to the east. Or perhaps it was a beetle on lightning feet, stomping across a valley. Every step was a boom, every footfall roared, and the ground leaped underfoot. This was faster than our trip here, when Phillius had gloated and danced with the love of speed. Madness chased us again, and from the captain's castle, Phillius sang of ladies and beer. He hummed the instrumental bits.

We ran south under all sail, and the end of the world pursued us.

As the Arsae lifted toward the Crests we slowed down, and goblins on the wide foothills of the towering cloud mountain hurled lassos. They wove the lightning into cords that shot from their hands to the ground, sometimes smashing taller branches and sometimes immolating the thyf. Masts on the *Dream in Emerald* were curiously slippery. Many times, the thunder reached for them, and I thought for sure we would be caught, but the lightning branched at the last moment, dancing overhead and diving into the sea beside us. Clockwork in the keel sang. Phillius began running side to side. The cloud was so many miles wide that attempting to get around it was impossible, but he made us a harder target. Deprived of our speed, we allowed fingers of rain to caress the deck. Phillius overloaded the sails to keep us going.

A bolt finally hit the starboard sails, burning through the sheets and snatching the sweeping mast in a burning grip. We jerked hard, side over side, and nearly crashed. Phillius dumped half our speed. Another lightning bolt snatched us from behind, laying down on the spar beside me and setting my hair on end. I dove back to the ship. Another and another line landed, and we were hooked.

"Boarding party!" screamed Aehr. The goblins leaped from cloud to lines of thunderbolts and slid down lightning on fine brass gauntlets.

"Glory," whispered Phillius. Othrak said, "Ah, freedom." The captain gave up the wheel and met the attackers.

Goblins outnumbered us and their long arms dwarfed the grip of the elves. They were bigger and stronger. They smashed Aehr and his scientists like adults beating children. Phillius was different. Pressures within him exploded at the instant of relaxation. His bare fingers stabbed flesh and skulls and peeled scalps like orange rinds. A Throathurter lifted him by the head and squeezed his neck until the veins bulged. Phillius dropped free when he cut the tendons of the goblin's arm with his bare hands. He leaped on the goblin and savaged his face with fine elvish teeth.

I don't really fight if I can avoid it, so when we fell into melee, I ran away. I threw myself below deck and toward the arcane clockwork engines that drove us. Here the light was dim and the footing terrible. Goblins came down to break the ship and charged the fine moving parts with fists raised. They did not succeed. It was dark down here, not the terrible, omnipotent dark of the shadows under Bloodharvest, but human dark, dark that spread like camouflage. In the shallow corridors of the hold, with lightning flashes all but relentless and unlit rooms impenetrable, I let the goblins come to me and dropped their bodies between the runners into the thyf. Long spider legs snatched the corpses into trees before they fell far, though I never saw a body.

"Elegy!" someone screamed above deck. "Elegy, I beg you!"

I stuck my head up and looked around.

The goblins had snatched Othrak and retreated. He writhed in their long-fingered hands as they scrambled up the lines to the thunderhead. Othrak bit and punched, but the rootwater hadn't reinvigorated him like it had the elves. He was half the weight of a small goblin, and his struggles were nothing but wind.

"Elegy, I beg you! We must remember him!" shouted Aehr.

I looked at him, the ship, and Phillius, who put us on a heading for the open sea, the rising Crests forming the southern horizon. They lifted up until the blue sky looked forever away. I hesitated.

"We will sing praises of you, Elegy. Your name will be a song of human greatness," begged Horase.

"My name *is* a song," I muttered, and ran after the goblins.

They were already on the thunderhead, and the thunderbolt boarding lines released their grip, snatching back to the cloud from whence they came. I stabbed one and rode it upward, holding the tiny handle of Luthas's knife with the blade lodged in plasma. There was nothing there, but that knife cut nothing. My feet left the deck and I shot into wind and rain and tumbled onto the cloud.

There was no deck. The cloud didn't have a top. The goblins had spun vapor into viscous air, a soft, yielding mass that settled underfoot. Staying still a moment made one sink, first slowly, then free falling. When I landed and rolled, the instant I tried to get my bearings almost dropped me to my doom. I had to spring upright and run, and there was never a chance to look around to see where I was going or plan a route. I had to move.

Goblins bore Othrak upward, climbing stairways gouged into the central tower of the thunderhead that rose toward the anvil. They were running scared. I chased after them. Here the cloud helped. It pushed my foot with every step, so I bounded up cliffs I could not climb, soaring distances I couldn't reach. Walls of lesser clouds broke before me. The goblins saw me, and they sent up a howling as they ran. There were many of them, but they fled the knife in my hands.

"Ghostheart!" they screamed. "Dread's wife!"

Actually, Maru Ghostheart had been Dread's concubine. His wife, Hodeiru Goldhead, had stayed back in Celephias. The goblins were being inaccurate. No one listened.

They crossed the top, and instants later I arrived as Othrak was hurled to the cloud before the storm cloud's captain. It was Laptra, master of Bloodharvest.

"Rumor had you dead," I said. I began to trot in a circle around her.

"Greatly exaggerated," she replied, turning to match me.

Othrak was slight enough to lay prone on the cloud. He scrabbled to get away but only kept his head above the cloud's thundering internals.

I shrugged. "I need that one alive."

"The one is mine! I killed his family to own him! I tortured their memory out of space and time so he would have nothing! I own that one!"

"Okay, devil goblin, I was being brief. His name is Othrak, and Othrak is coming with me." I picked my trot up to a run, still circling.

"Never!" She matched me again.

Laptra was a big one, and they're faster than humans are, even for their size. It's the way their joints are hinged. Laptra carried one of the terrible goblin swords of Whitehall, Omen, a hungry blade of gray brass. Where a western sword might have hamon, this one carried the cloud-wave pattern in mixed silver and steel. We circled Othrak while around us the goblins whispered and capered, keeping their feet moving.

"You fool," I said. I pulled my cloak around me. "I have made terrible deals with the shadows under Bloodharvest. I have spoken the names of Dread and unleashed faceless despair." The truth of the words hit the watchers hard, and they recoiled. Laptra didn't. "I have cut through nightmares. I wield the Blade of Luthas, a stardagger that leaves cuts in the stuff of the world so the outer darkness can look in! I have claimed ownership of Othrak, and you defy me? When I cut you, the Mad Drummer himself will look into your heart!" My hand flashed under the cloak.

Omen soared from its sheath as Laptra lunged to parry, and the blade of Whitehall cut my broken, water-logged lantern in half. She doused herself in oil. I threw a fistful of firepaper and bells after the lantern. Soaked, she burst into flame among the jingling ring. It sounded like a holiday. I grabbed Othrak and ran.

More specifically, I fell miles upon miles straight down, kicking and shoving at nothing but cloud to keep us moving toward the edge. There was stuff in here; weak, ethereal stuff, but stuff none the less, and the cloud pushed back. We broached the south side of the thunderhead, where a few goblins still maintained ranks at the lightning hawsers. I threatened them with the knife. Goblins dove to get out of my way as I stole a lightning bolt.

I landed on the *Dream in Emerald* in thunder and pain, and dropped Othrak at Aehr's feet. With a twist of the blade of Luthas I cut free the lightning, and it fizzled away.

"You tell your Mom—" I yelled at him, and had to pause because I forgot what I was going to say. "You tell her this isn't cheap!"

I had something here. Options? Was it options? The moment passed.

With Phillius at the helm, we sailed south to the Crests. The thunderhead lurched north from where it was, and before going a mile began to wither. Goblins tumbled out of the sky and fell into the Arsae, making only splashes in thyf.

Elegy is staying in Pallas
and will return for her next contract.

Get updates at my blog:
www.leibnizclockwork.com

www.ingramcontent.com/pod-product-compliance
Lightning Source LLC
Chambersburg PA
CBHW030551130626
46552CB00006B/2502